Moo

Santa & Pete: a novel of
Christmas past ans present

SANTA & PETE

A Novel of
Christmas Present and Past

**Christopher Moore and
Pamela Johnson**

Illustrations by Julie Scott

Simon & Schuster

SIMON & SCHUSTER
Rockefeller Center
1230 Avenue of the Americas
New York, NY 10020

Designed by Katy Riegel

Manufactured in the United States of America
1   3   5   7   9   10   8   6   4   2

Library of Congress Cataloging-in-Publication Data
Moore, Christopher.
Santa & Pete : a novel of Christmas present and past / Christopher Moore and Pamela
Johnson : illustrations by Julie Scott.
p.   cm.
1. Afro-Americans—New York (State)—New York—Fiction.
2. Christmas—New York (State)—New York—Fiction.
3. Santa Claus—Fiction. I. Johnson, Pamela. II. Title.
PS3563.05935S26   1998
813'.54—dc21   98-27776
CIP

ISBN 0-684-85495-3

Fic 11-5-08
Xmas

Acknowledgments

*F*OR HELPING SANTA AND PETE to fly, we warmly thank Laurie Chittenden, Janet Hill, Victoria Sanders, Scott Waxman, and Carlene Bauer.

Pamela Johnson is deeply appreciative of Cheo Tyehimba, Rosemarie Robotham, Patrick Henry Bass, and the Essence Family.

Christopher Moore gratefully and lovingly acknowledges Swartine, Captain Jan DeVries, Dominie Bogardus, Janetje Roosevelt, Nancy and Harvey Moore, Norma K. DeFreese Moore, Hillburn, Pine Bush, Arthur Schomburg, Ken Gorsuch, Kim Yancey Moore, Terence, and all who follow.

In memory of my grandcestors, Maria Angola and Emmanuel "Big Man" Angola, who arrived in the New World from Africa c. 1626, and Nicholas "Little Man" Manuel, who was baptized August 22, 1649, in New Amsterdam at the Church of Saint Nicholas. And to its Dutch motto: Eendracht maakt macht—Unity makes strength.

–Christopher Moore

For Joyce and Oliver, my mamacita and papasan. For Keren, my little sis. And for Harlem, my birthplace and my home.

–Pamela Johnson

The Ornament

THE MOMENT I OPEN the delicate tissue protecting the first ornament, I feel a rush of Christmas spirit. The little yellow bus with tiny faces peering out of every window doesn't look at all like the one my grandfather drove through the streets of New York City for nearly thirty years, but I chose it to represent him because he schooled me on the finer points of love and life.

We keep the tiny bus in one of our three boxes of "grandcestor" ornaments. Every December, my wife Cassandra, our children Maria and Manuel, and I bring the boxes up from the basement to our living room. As we unpack them one by one, we remember the name and contribution of each of our relatives before placing their ornament on the Christmas tree. Slowly but surely, we transform the fragrant pine branches into our family tree.

A tiny gourd painted with brilliant flashes of color represents our fiery foremother Maria; she came to America from Angola, with a long layover in Holland. The hand-carved pipe is for Big Manuel, her husband, who loved to whittle. Maria and Big Man are from my side of the family. For twelve generations now, we've passed down our history by word of mouth and written it on the inside covers of family Bibles.

When Cassandra first suggested that we create an ancestor ritual for the holidays, she was frustrated because she knew only that her grandparents had come north to Harlem from Alabama and Virginia in the 1920s. It was on her sixteenth birthday that her mother, Mattie Mills, gave her a pair of train tickets from 1921 and told her of the migration, along with all she knew of the family story.

A few years ago, when Cassandra decided she wanted to dig deeper, we packed the kids up for a summer vacation and took a train down South, stopping in Richmond and Mobile, to try to learn more about her grandparents and great-grands. Along the way, we discovered bits and pieces of her history, but our biggest find was that she'd had a great-great-grandmother named Eliza, who had lived and died a slave on a tobacco plantation in Richmond. Imagine

Eliza picking the wide, dark leaves and stuffing them into a scratchy burlap sack as she toiled from can see to can't—as they described those days in the fields that started at sunrise and ended well after sunset. We figure she wore a straw hat to protect her head from the scalding sun, but on our tree she's symbolized by a tiny white bonnet like the one we imagine she'd have worn when she got herself all dressed up for Sunday worship.

We've laminated Cassandra's grandparents' old train tickets from Richmond to New York City, and carefully placed a hook through the reinforced edge of the plastic border. Now they, too, hang on the tree, along with another pair of ticket stubs from a 1926 dance at the Renaissance Ballroom over on 138th Street in Harlem. Before they closed the old dance hall down, Cassandra's grandparents could be found there most Saturday evenings, dancing as if it were the last night on earth.

Reminiscing like this, we unpack the ornaments one by one; we go on through the generations—and down the Christmas tree—until all our known ancestors have joined us. Sometimes toward the end of the evening our children start to get sleepy, but they snap awake the moment we open the final box and unveil the miniature figurines of Santa and Pete.

Cassandra, who is a professional potter, cast the two ornaments

The Ornament

herself from porcelain. Santa is rosy-cheeked, wearing the familiar crimson coat and coal-colored boots, while Pete has a lean, chiseled black face, framed by a white turban, and wears a long brown tunic. Though born in Spain, Pete had roots that stretched back to the sprawling deserts of northern Africa.

When company visits during the holidays, they're instantly intrigued by him. They want to know who he is, and how he earned a spot right next to Santa at the top of our Christmas tree. Of course I want to tell them right away, but Cassandra and the kids always insist that the story be the finale to our annual holiday party.

So after a few cookies, we invite our guests to settle around the fireplace, and then I start the story of Santa and Pete. Everyone knows Santa. Many even know his real name is St. Nicholas, and that he was born a good 1,600 years before the first shopping mall. Fewer, however, know that he was a Christian bishop who traveled the world performing small miracles.

As for Pete, history nearly leaves him out altogether. There's very little written of men like him, known as Moors, who came over from Africa and Arabia to rule Spain and parts of Portugal, France, and Italy for seven centuries. They were mostly Moslems. And many were scholars, studying literature, geography, and mathematics.

Of Pete, we know only that he was born a slave on a farm in

Spain. In his youth, he taught animals to do amazing tricks without ever taking a whip to them. And he could plow the fields with a team of oxen faster than anyone. He was so enterprising that by the time he was eighteen, he'd earned enough money to buy his freedom. He left the farm and ventured into the forest to commune with God and to study the heavens so that he might learn to navigate the earth. At night when he gazed at the sky, he felt especially close to the Creator, because he believed that God had planted a twinkling seed of inspiration in each star. Whenever he encountered a problem, he imagined it surrounded by stardust, and a solution came to him.

After a year of contemplation in the forest, Pete sought work in Seville, where he took a job as a cook in a prison. They hired him not only because he could prepare meals quickly, but also because he could coax so many bowls of soup from one kettle that it seemed bottomless.

One day, when he was out shopping for soup fixings, he happened upon a blind woman with a scarf tied under her chin. She sat under an olive tree, playing her lute. Pete stood there quietly, reveling in the enchanting swirl of sounds. Then, without warning, the woman stopped in the middle of her song, held the lute out in Pete's direction, and said, "Take it and go." He stepped forward and kissed her cheek in thanks, too stunned to say a word, and then turned and headed for home.

Though Seville surrounded him in Spanish music spiked with African and Arabic rhythms, Pete's own plucking of the strings produced notes and chords that crashed around his feet like falling stars. And yet, whenever he took a break from work, he would find a place to practice, eager to recapture the blind woman's magic. But even with his music and his cherished books, Pete felt he lacked a mission worthy of God's favor.

Religion was central to everyday life in the Old World. Yet people of differing faiths often clashed, and sometimes their conflicts turned deadly. Even the Moors, who were considered tolerant of those holding other beliefs, had their share of zealots. And one day, a Moorish prince, who knew of St. Nick's pilgrimages, singled him out for persecution.

It wasn't long before St. Nick wound up in the same Seville prison where Pete worked. St. Nick had been making his annual pilgrimage from the Holy Land to Holland when he was captured, accused of spying, and sentenced to die the very next morning. Though he had all the faith in the world, he had never been so frightened. In the moment that the prison bars slammed in his face, God's grace seemed just beyond his reach.

Pete had been preparing that evening's meal when the new prisoners arrived, but later, as he passed out bowls of chicken soup, he found himself lingering by St. Nick's cell door. Something about St. Nick's presence inspired him. To Peter, St. Nick's face appeared to be encircled in stardust.

Later, Pete came back after his appointed rounds, and the two men talked through the iron bars. When St. Nick shivered with cold, Pete gave him a blanket. When the old man seemed frightened and alone, Pete slipped him a volume of spiritual verse. And that's how they passed the long, dark hours until dawn.

The next morning, when the executioners came for St. Nick, they found both men gone. A light snow had fallen overnight, but there were no tracks. Later, people near Spain's northern coast reported having seen two shepherds—one white, one black—making their way toward the place where the ships sail for Holland.

In that country, St. Nick was the national saint, and the people all drew on his spirit. Every December 6, they held a feast in his honor. For several hundred years after St. Nick met Pete, around the year 1000, they made the annual pilgrimage to Holland together. For many years, they disguised themselves so they could slip through Spain and arrive in Amsterdam for the early December celebration.

One year, St. Nick and Pete left Holland and set sail for America. . . . But I'm jumping ahead of myself. The reason I know this story at all is because my grandfather treasured history enough to share it with me. At the time, I was a little boy who preferred flying kites to spending the day listening to an old man. But I grew to love his stories. Now I face the same battle for attention with my own children. I hope that one day they'll come to value life, love, faith, forgiveness, and a playful sense of humor more than anything you could fit under a tree. These are the gifts Santa and Pete began delivering a thousand years ago. They shared them with our ancestors, who handed them down to us. So this is my tale of Christmas present and past—it's a gift for you, and for generations to come.

$Getting\ to$
$Know\ Him$

$\mathcal{J}$ WAS ONLY SEVEN when my grandfather told me this story for the first time. My parents had decided to send me out with him each Saturday morning. As a city bus driver, he looped around Manhattan's twelve miles again and again, giving his passengers a running commentary on all the changes this island city has seen over the centuries. His ancestors—African, Indian, and Dutch—had settled Manhattan long ago, and he loved to tell about it. Initially I thought it would be pure torture to sit still all day listening to a never-ending history lesson. I remember grumbling when my mother first told me of the plan. She came to my room on a Friday evening before dinner, as I sat amid the ever-present clutter.

Getting to Know Him

"Your father and I want you to get to know him better. He is your only living grandparent," she explained as she surveyed the chaos with her arms folded across her chest. Clearly, my room was nowhere near as clean as I'd claimed when I'd talked her into letting me play outside for an extra half hour. Though still in her twenties, my mother wore her long black hair in a bun, and her cat-eye glasses low on her button nose. She worked as a librarian at the Countee Cullen branch of the New York Public Library. That, her way with crossword puzzles, and her huge vocabulary had me convinced that she was the smartest person on the planet.

"What more do I need to know about him?" I asked her, trying to kick a couple of toys under the bed with the back of my heel. I had zero interest in their babysitting plan, figuring my grandfather didn't know a thing about boys my age. Not that he was a mean man. In fact, people throughout the neighborhood praised his kindness and his willingness to lend a hand. He often showed up at a new neighbor's home with his toolbox, helping to transform many a dilapidated brownstone into an urban palace. But to spend every Saturday with him? Since church took up most of Sunday, I wouldn't have enough time over the weekend to play with my friends!

I hadn't spent much time alone with my grandfather, though he and my grandmother had visited our home often when I was younger. They brought a lot of laughter with them, although they sometimes joked that they had to "hold hands to keep from fighting." My grandmother died when I was five, and a sadness rushed in and claimed my grandfather. Without laughter, his towering stature intimidated me and his thunderous voice made me quake.

"There's plenty you don't know about him," my mother told me, watching my crafty footwork without comment. "And some things I'm sure he'd like to know about you. So if it's okay with you, then, you'll ride with him tomorrow."

I sat there stumped for a moment. I wanted to tell her that my friend Basil and I were supposed to fly kites the next day. Or maybe I could tell her that I had a stomachache that I was certain would stretch well into the next week. Or I could just tell her the truth: that my grandfather made me nervous.

"Just don't tell him about my room," I yelled out as her shoes clicked against the hardwood floor all the way down the hall.

"Then clean it up," she yelled back laughing.

Santa & Pete

THE NEXT MORNING, as my parents fixed breakfast, I eavesdropped on their conversation from my favorite hiding place under the stairwell. It was the cubbyhole where I kept my marbles and my Broadway program from *A Raisin in the Sun.* I liked to sit there, listen in, and pick up good gossip—although I was often at a loss to make any sense of it.

This particular morning, however, as my father scraped butter across a slice of toast and Miles Davis's "Sketches of Spain" played in the background, I learned two things. First, our roof needed to be replaced, and second, my parents' decision to match up my grandfather and me was more for his benefit than for mine. As I listened, they went on about my grandmother's passing, and my grandfather's lingering grief.

"All he does is work," my mother said. "He didn't even come to Thanksgiving dinner because he volunteered to cover someone else's shift. It's like he's avoiding the holidays and family altogether." Still shaken by her mother's death, she seemed worried that she was losing her father, too.

Getting to Know Him

I heard the spatula tapping the plates and imagined them loaded with bacon, eggs, and toast. When hunger finally snared me into the kitchen from my perch, my parents both looked at me silently, then each of them tripped over the other asking me if I was excited about spending the day with my grandfather.

What could I say after everything I'd heard? I wasn't thrilled. But my grandfather needed me—and I needed a few things from Santa. With Christmas only four weeks away, this was no time to mess up.

"My Copilot"

 $\mathcal{I}$ T WAS A CRISP Saturday morning in late November 1959 when my mother tightened the belt of her white robe with the pink rosebuds, threw a coat over it, and then bundled me up too. Together, we walked hand in hand along the row of brownstone stoops to the bus stop a half block down from our home.

The boulevard before us was grand, boasting architecture lush with Old World crests, regal faces, and fancy garlands. Many of the men and women walking up and down the street wore hats and gloves and pants with crisp creases. Even my mother cut a sharp profile in her trench coat, cinched at the waist. I'm sure no one suspected the nightclothes or the worry underneath.

"I don't know what kind of Christmas we're going to have this year, Terence," she said. She looked down at me apologetically. Her face was a smooth honey-brown oval. She looked a lot like her father. And I looked like her.

"What's the matter?" I asked. "Is Santa sick?"

"It's not that. It's that we have to replace the roof."

"You worried about Santa landing on it?"

"Not exactly," she said, letting the words fade.

Money was always tight around our house—even when my father had a long-running gig at a jazz club in Greenwich Village. Basil's father had been out of work for a while. He and a lot of other folks were boycotting some of the white stores on 125th Street because they didn't want to hire blacks. Even as a boy I realized times were hard everywhere, and scary too, as black people and white people argued and sometimes came to blows over how to share America.

Before more could be said, we'd arrived at the stop. I squinted through the sunshine up St. Nicholas Avenue, looking for a two-tone green southbound bus that I hoped would never come. Moments later, I saw it, and then, suddenly—faster than you can say "Flash Gordon"—my grandfather had arrived. He stopped exactly before us, and then opened the door by pushing out a lever like the punching right hook of a Rock 'em Sock 'em Robot. He looked proud and official in his blue uniform, tiny waves of silver hair flowing between his cap and collar.

"There's my copilot," he said in his booming voice as I slowly climbed up the bus steps, unsure of what should come next. That's when my mother, who followed me up, kissed him, turned and kissed me, and then gave me a secret push forward so that I would kiss him too. Then she rushed back down the steps and turned quickly toward me.

"Be good," she said in that no-nonsense tone she used when I was to follow her instructions to a T. I watched through the bus window as she ran back to our house; I felt abandoned.

"Grab a seat, son." My grandfather's voice rattled me as he signaled with his chin toward a brown vinyl bench opposite his seat. A second later we were off.

I looked around the nearly empty bus as I felt my pockets for the toys I'd stuffed into them: a yo-yo, a few tiger-eye marbles, and a rubberband-bound deck of Yankees player cards. My Willie Mays card topped them all, even though he played for the Giants. He was my hero. I tried to copy his cool "basket catch"—the way he scooped up the ball right at his waist like it was no sweat.

I brought along as many distractions as I could, since boredom almost always got me in trouble. How long, I wondered, would it be before I did something that riled my grandfather? My parents lasted about twenty minutes. I looked at my grandfather's thick eyebrows and high, hollowed cheeks, and gave it a half hour.

"How you been keeping, son?" He stared at my newsboy cap until I took it off.

"Fine."

"Sure are getting big."

"I drink milk," I said.

He laughed, then popped a couple of fresh-shelled peanuts into his mouth, red-paper skin and all. I didn't know it at the time, but he made it a policy to keep at least a couple of clusters in his jacket pockets at all times.

"You know," he said as he tapped the pedal, giving the engine a dose of gas, "St. Nicholas Avenue—this route we're traveling right now—used to be an Indian trail.

"And used to be that if you craned your neck just right, you could look down this hill all the way to St. Nicholas Church in lower Manhattan. That's where your first ancestors were baptized," my grandfather told me as we chugged along in the light Saturday traffic.

"Let you in on another little-known fact." He was having fun now. I studied his large, well-manicured hands as they commanded the steering wheel. Basil was probably threading his kite and testing the wind by now.

"'Bout three hundred years ago," my grandfather went on, "Wall Street wasn't even a street—just a wooden wall about ten feet tall that stretched from the east to the west at the northern edge of the colony. Part of the reason they built it was to keep the Indians out. The Empire State Building and the Statue of Liberty?" He glanced over at me. "Didn't exist." Then he proceeded to erase the city I had just begun to discover, as he put in its place a dusty old town called New Amsterdam.

"Why'd they want to keep the Indians out?" I asked, mildly curious.

"That's a long story, son," he said. "But we'll get to it."

As we continued along the route, I began to think my parents were right: my grandfather was pretty bad off. He talked on and on, pointing out people and places just outside his window. The only trouble was that they flat-out weren't there, like windmills at Macy's department store, or a frozen lake full of skaters where a row of court buildings clearly stood. When he spoke of people like my grandmother or ancestors from long ago, it was as if they were still alive. Right then and there, I figured that I should listen a little more closely so I could warn somebody if I thought the old man was really about to snap.

When he finally dropped me off at home late that afternoon, my ears buzzed. As he walked me up the steps to the house, I scanned the sidewalk for Basil, but he had gone in already. The sky mixed purples and oranges and the streetlights flickered on, which meant it was too late to play outside.

My father opened the door with a big broad grin, but I flew under his arm.

"Goodnight, son," my grandfather yelled up to me as I reached the top of the stairs.

" 'Night," I shouted back.

On the Road
Again

No AMOUNT of persuading or pleading on my part seemed to shake my parents from the notion that these Saturday adventures weren't the best thing since meatloaf and red gravy.

So the next week there I was, getting on the bus again, trying not to think about how time crawls when you're stuck somewhere you don't want to be. That's when I noticed something that I hadn't picked up on before: As passengers waited at the stops, some waved on the bus ahead of us, even though it was going to the same destination as my grandfather's bus. Then they'd flag him down. And when they got on, a number of them greeted my grandfather by name, gathering in the seats nearest to his, even though there was plenty of room throughout the bus. My grandfather seemed to know their names too: Mrs. McCloud, Professor DeFreese, Maya, Mr. Levinson and his granddaughter Rachel. Sometimes they would stay on long past their stop if he'd started a good story.

"Morning, Mr. Mann," said a petite blond woman with round, rimless spectacles as she rushed up the steps and deposited her fare. "See you've got your grandson with you again. He's still as handsome as last week."

"Say thank you to Professor DeFreese, son."

I mumbled a thanks. But she had dashed on to another subject.

"Headed back to New Amsterdam today?" she asked, smiling.

"Feel like making that trek?" he asked.

"Well, you know my parents were Dutch, so I always like to hear more about the place," she replied, as she sat in the first row of forward-facing seats behind my grandfather, and diagonally across from me. Then she turned to me and smiled. I noticed one of her front teeth overlapped the other.

"Professor DeFreese," my grandfather said, calling over his shoulder before pulling back into traffic, "you ever hear of an African bird called Sankofa?"

"Can't say that I have, Mr. Mann," she replied.

I hadn't either.

On the Road Again

"It's a mythic bird that seems to fly forward while looking back. The point being that if you know where you come from, you have a better sense of where you need to go."

"Sankofa," she said slowly, as though the word tasted sweet.

Look backward and see where you're headed? At the time, it seemed crazy to me, but I was beginning to realize that people listened to my grandfather. Professor DeFreese and the others rode his bus every Saturday, coming aboard and taking the same seats as the week before, leaning in to hear him like children during story hour. And my grandfather delivered.

"Walking into New Amsterdam might be like walking into your own house and not recognizing the place. Like somebody took all the furniture out, made the walls stone, and the floors dirt. . . ."

Grandpa didn't use a lot of thees and thous, but his voice sounded different, more formal, as if he might have lived back then himself. His tone transported us. And we were soon looking into the clear eyes of a Lenape Indian woman as she used a sharpened stone to clean the sticky insides of beaver pelts before spreading them out to dry in the sun. Then she and her husband gathered the skins to trade with the European sailors who, at first, only passed through. We heard the almost-dead-sounding warble of an African slave as he sang to blot out the pain in his arms, while sawing down

200-foot maple and oak trees so the town could grow. And we imagined the anguished face of a Dutchwoman stealing one last glance at Holland as she crowded onto a ship, prepared to live her life in a place that she had never laid eyes on. Through Grandpa our ancestors became living, breathing people.

Grandpa would talk for a while, then get quiet, as if he was letting us soak it all in. Those were the eerie moments when I used to think one of his characters might walk right out of history and onto our bus.

"So what was *this*, Grandpa?" I asked, looking out the window at Greenwich Village, where my father often played his saxophone in the neighborhood jazz clubs.

"This area's near where your African ancestors live," he said, still speaking as if the past were the present. "Only they call it the Greenwood, because of the huge evergreens and all the plants and grasses that sprout up near the swamp."

How could he see greenery, when I saw concrete, and how could he see a swamp on a day that was dry as a bone?

Grandpa pointed out Stone Street, the island's first paved road, and sure enough, cobblestones rippled out before us. He told us that Pearl Street got its name for the oyster shells people tossed over their shoulders as they ate "take-out" from the mouth of the Hudson

River. The street called Maiden Lane? Grandpa said that young, single women washed their laundry at the end of it—right in the East River—and listened to all the boys' tired pickup lines.

As Grandpa went on, I realized that the most casual things, like a street name, could have a wealth of history behind them. Every step I took, someone had walked there before me. Maybe the footsteps belonged to my ancestors or maybe somebody like Marcus Garvey or Harriet Tubman, I thought. And if one of my feet touched the same place where one of theirs had once been, I wondered whether I could tap the same power and vision that had made them great.

"Ain't nobody lived on this island longer than your folks, son," Grandpa said, pulling me out of my daydream. "Your family's been here a dozen generations. And considering your Indian roots, how far back could that reach? Maybe a few thousand years?"

He peeked over at me to see if I was as pleased with that information as he was.

For some reason I couldn't grasp at the time, I sat up straighter. I didn't feel quite as alone or insignificant. But what did it all mean, and what did my ancestors' lives have to do with mine?

"You haven't talked about the part where the Dutch supposedly bought Manhattan for $24 in beads," said Professor DeFreese.

"And you know how that story ends," Maya said. Her favorite seat, when it was available, was directly behind my grandfather. And that's where she sat as she looked at Professor DeFreese as if it were Maya's very own land that had been lost. Maybe Maya, with her wide, brown face, had descended from the Lenape like the woman in Grandpa's tale.

"The Dutch got a real steal," Maya said sadly, "but the Indians found themselves put out of their own home. Can you imagine? They thought the Dutch just wanted to use the land while they were passing through, so why not share? I mean, who can really own an island? It's like claiming the moon. It's God's property."

"The Dutch were a lot more concrete about things," Professor DeFreese told her, adjusting her round, gold-rimmed glasses. "More dollars-and-cents people. They definitely did some things that were wrong, but a big part of it was a clash of cultures."

Maya and Professor DeFreese seemed wary of each other, and it made me uneasy. My grandfather couldn't see them, but I imagined that he could feel the heat. Mr. Levinson, who sat between them, seemed on edge too, tapping his cane again and again as if he were trying to slowly punch a hole through the floor.

"People think every issue is about race," he huffed under his breath.

"Who was right, Grandpa, the Indians or the Dutch?" I asked.

"Depends on who's telling the story," he said, laughing to himself. "I'll let you puzzle it out. But it wasn't just race that divided people, son," Grandpa said. "It was religion, too."

"I was wondering when you were going to say something about the religious intolerance, because there was plenty," Mr. Levinson said, sounding off again. At that his granddaughter, wedged between him and Maya, began to twirl a lock of hair anxiously.

Only Mrs. McCloud, who wore fancy church hats—today's being peach with over-the-eye netting—seemed content. But then anything my grandfather said might move her to laugh and clap her gloved hands lightly. She preferred the first forward-facing seat just behind me. I knew from the moment I saw her look at my grandfather that she had a crush on him. I was worried that she would come between me and him.

"Okay over there, Mrs. McCloud?" Grandpa asked.

"Just fine, Mr. Mann," she purred.

We rode along for a while with no one saying anything, no one even making eye contact. Boredom ran toward me with open arms. I started to doze off.

"Got to show you my basement museum one day." Grandpa's voice roused me. I saw him toss back a couple of peanuts. "Been meaning to take you, but since your Grandma got sick . . ." His voice choked up for a moment, then slowly cleared. Though he only lived around the corner from us, I hadn't been to his house in a long, long time.

"Yep, I got to take you down there. Got a wooden sign, almost three hundred years old, from when they spelled Harlem with two As. Used to be nailed to a tree right at the border of Haarlem Village, just on the Post Road. Got some flint arrowheads from the Indians, even got the 'free papers' of an ex-slave named Mary Gunderson. She carried them everywhere so that people wouldn't try to force her back into her old 'job.' Ain't no fun working for no pay—especially when your boss is an ungrateful so-and-so trying to whip your hindparts all the time." At that, he let out a big, rumbling laugh.

I laughed too. So did Mrs. McCloud. Then Rachel, Maya, Professor DeFreese, and finally Mr. Levinson. It seemed to ease the strain a little bit, at least for the moment.

"Wow, you got your own museum," I said. I wasn't wild about museums. Even today I'll take a live-action flick over a dead impressionist's painting, but somehow, even at seven years old, I sensed that there would be something special in Grandpa's museum. A fragment of who he was and maybe who we all were.

"Wow, your own museum," I said again, wanting him to know I was impressed.

He smiled. I smiled too. And to this day, I remember that moment as distinct from all the rest.

HE HAD A SHORT BREAK before we started back uptown. All the passengers had been delivered to their destinations, so after stopping the bus, Grandpa got up and sat next to me. We ate peanut-butter-and-jelly sandwiches and drank chocolate milk, which my mother had packed for us. Across the way, we watched scores of people boarding the boats bound for the Statue of Liberty.

Grandpa pointed over to the other side of the street. He said it used to be Fort Amsterdam, the original Dutch settlement. Inside its walls were a governor's mansion, soldiers' barracks, and the first St. Nicholas Church. But all I saw was a block-long building that looked like a bank.

So much had changed. Everybody seemed to be in a hurry to make progress, but Grandpa liked the old stuff. He fussed at my parents for selling off their antique furniture, scoffed at food from cans and freezers, and preferred his radio to almost anything on TV. His highest praise was "Now, that's the real McCoy!" Grandpa didn't even want to forget about slavery—he seemed to feel that we would all need to hold on to those memories to remind us how important it was to stay free.

"If you know all this history," I asked him, "why do you drive a bus?"

"I'd like to think of myself as a roving historian, son. I help people to see things they might have missed," he said, wiping a crumb from my lips.

"Way back when, this job looked pretty good. Got me and your grandmother a house and put two girls through college. So you might say I just bloomed where I was planted."

"But you could write history books," I told him, suddenly sad that he spent his days driving around in circles. "Ones that actually keep people awake."

"I'm more of a talker than a writer," Grandpa said.

"Somebody could write all that stuff down for you," I suggested.

Grandpa looked at me for a moment. "Maybe one day they will, son. Maybe whoever does it will even put in a line or two about your old grandpa."

"One more question."

"Shoot," Grandpa said.

"Why do you call me son when my name is Terence?"

"I never had a son," he told me. "I kind of liked the idea. But I can call you Terence."

"No," I said. "Call me son."

A T   H O M E   L A T E R   that evening, I asked my mother about Grandpa's stories.

"He used to tell me the same tales he's telling you," she said as she stirred a frozen brick of spinach into a small saucepan. "Too bad I wouldn't sit still long enough to listen."

Just then my father walked in, sat down, and rested his arms against our white kitchen table with blue trim. He had panda eyebrows that made him look a little tired, and muttonchop sideburns, which he trimmed religiously. I played with my knife and fork as my mother and father launched into a discussion that floated from civil rights to the Russians' strides in space to whether we could afford a summer vacation.

On the Road Again

"Excuse me," I interrupted, "but I have to know. Did all that stuff Grandpa talked about really happen?"

"Well, yes," my mother said, sliding on an oven mitt and reaching in for the meatloaf. Then she tilted the pan and ladled a ketchup-y sauce over the meat. "You think your grandfather would drive around all day inventing a bunch of nonsense? Do yourself a favor and pay attention," she told me, sliding a plate of food in front of me. "He'll give you the skinny you can't find in so-called history books."

"Your grandpa's really good," my father chimed in. "We especially like how he gets you out of our hair every Saturday," he said laughing.

"I knew it from the very beginning!" I looked back and forth between my parents.

"James," my mother fussed at my father, a giggle quivering at the corners of her mouth, "quit hectoring that boy so he can eat."

In It Together

WEEK AFTER WEEK, my grandfather added layers to his tale. I began to look forward to the moment when he pulled up to the stop and I ran up the stairs of his bus.

As we rolled along, I discovered that Manhattan has a spine like a dinosaur's—tallest at the top, and then tapering down. Numbered streets cross wide avenues, until you get to the bottom, where New Amsterdam used to be. There it still seems quaint, like a town where they paved a street or built a house as it was needed, with no bigger plan in mind.

At 181st Street, near the rocky top of Manhattan, we always picked up Mr. Levinson and his granddaughter Rachel. Without fail, he wore black, and he relied on his cane on his left side and on her on his right. She had thick brown hair, scooped up in a pony-tail, and wide-open eyes, as if something had just startled her. One day, Grandpa suggested that Mr. Levinson walked like the governor of New Amsterdam, Peter Stuyvesant, whose leg got blown off by a cannon during a battle and was replaced by a wooden peg.

At 135th Street, which was lined with neighborhood businesses, Mrs. McCloud, aka the Hat Lady, joined us. Grandpa told me she looked like our foremother Maria. Further down, Professor DeFreese lived in one of the high-rises near where she boarded at 96th Street. She always ran up the steps out of breath, one of her shoulders loaded down by a canvas bag full of papers. Grandpa said she might have been mistaken for Janet Roosevelt, the ancestor of two American presidents.

At 86th, another shopping district, we picked up Maya. She usually boarded with a half loaf of bread still in the colorful Wonder bread bag en route to Battery Park, all the way downtown, to feed the birds. So of course, in my mind, I nicknamed her the Bird Lady. But Grandpa said she resembled a magical Indian woman named Ramapo, who sneaked into New Amsterdam one day when the village was on the brink of war.

Each Saturday, the regulars brought me Cracker Jacks and Matchbox cars, pinching my cheek or squeezing my shoulder as they got on. There was still a little tension between Maya and Professor DeFreese, while Mr. Levinson continued to grumble about parts of the story he thought my grandfather left out. And yet, together we all listened, going further and further back in time, until we arrived at the day when Santa and Pete first set foot in New Amsterdam.

"Yep," Grandpa said, that mid-December morning, delivering the baited hook to my cheek, "New Amsterdam didn't know what hit it when Santa and Pete arrived. They even met some of your ancestors."

"Santa Claus met *my* ancestors?" I asked him.

"And don't forget Pete," he said.

"Who's Pete?" Rachel asked.

Professor DeFreese looked up. Then Maya tuned in. You know Mrs. McCloud was paying rapt attention, so that left Mr. Levinson, who had been tapping his cane but slowly turned his head toward Grandpa too.

"Curious, right?" Grandpa smiled as he let a couple of passengers off, and we began moving again.

I waited and waited for him to get on with the story, but he didn't.

"You're all gonna have to wait to hear the Santa and Pete story," he told us. "I only tell that one once a year."

We all groaned.

"When?" someone asked.

"Soon," he said.

"One minute is gonna come 'soon,'" I reminded him. "Then will you tell it?"

"No. Not then."

"What about in an hour?"

"Not then either. Just sit tight, son."

So I looked out the window and started counting blue cars. It calmed me, and to this day when I am on the verge of losing my cool, I will find something to count—cars, fingers, the moons of Jupiter—until the moment passes.

But back then, I didn't know from cool. So the next day, I called my grandfather, as I did two or three times daily throughout that week. When I got him on the line, I had only two words for him:

Who's Pete?

He seemed really glad to hear from me, and went on talking about everything under the sun, never getting around to my question. And no amount of calling or pestering unlocked his jaws.

When I asked him when he would tell me the story, he just replied, "Soon."

"When?" I'd ask again.

"Soon." He seemed content to repeat it as many times as it took for me to get it.

"How long?" I asked again.

"Not long," he said, offering a slight twist on the refrain.

Snowflakes Like Silver Dollars

WHEN GRANDPA arrived at my stop Christmas Eve morning, he had decorated his bus. A pine wreath with a large red bow sprouted from the front bumper, and inside, along the windows, hung waves of fringy gold garland. When I ran up the steps, he gave me a big smile and a tiny red-and-green candy cane. I gave him a kiss. Right away, I noticed something different. He'd pasted a newspaper article on the narrow, see-through wall behind his seat. The *Amsterdam News* had featured him a couple of days before in a long article, and they'd run his picture to boot. Famous Harlem photographer James VanDerZee had taken the shot. The headline read:

JOURNEY TO THE PAST
FOR ONLY FIFTEEN CENTS

"That's pretty cool, Grandpa." I admired the picture of him looking back like a Sankofa bird as he climbed the steps of his own bus. "That's sure a nice picture of you. How about we drive to the past and see if we run into Santa and Pete?"

"Grab a seat, son," he said, pointing with his chin to my usual spot near the door.

I settled there, fumbling with a new yo-yo, grabbing a few more toys from my pocket. As I pulled off my coat, the yo-yo fell, and I lunged after it.

"Got to sit down, son," he warned me again. "If I stop short you might go flying through the window. Who do you think you are, Rudi the red-nosed reindeer?" Then he winked at me, and I giggled.

"Although with those antlers on your head," he added, "you could pass for Rudi."

"It's Rudolph, Grandpa," I said, feeling around my head for any signs of reindeerdom but coming up empty-handed.

Mr. Levinson grumbled a brief hello as he got on. But Rachel boarded with a cheery "Merry Christmas and Happy Hanukkah,

Mr. Mann and Terence." She brought Grandpa a tin of something wrapped in a big red bow.

Mrs. McCloud came bearing a gift as well. She stepped up as if she had springs in her soles, and deposited her fare in the box. She set a shopping bag near Grandpa's seat as he pulled off from the curb.

"Brought you something I made," she said, her voice a hair above a whisper, as if it were a secret between her and him. Today's hat was yellow and satiny with shell-shaped yellow netting over her eyes. She looked—as usual—as if she had a fancy party to attend. The open shopping bag sent a warm, sweet aroma my way. I imagined it was a cake or a batch of butter cookies. As copilot, I thought I should have first crack at the goods, but I counted cars instead.

Grandpa thanked Rachel and Mrs. McCloud, placing Rachel's tin in the shopping bag.

After we'd picked up the regulars, who all brought gifts, a big smile spread across Grandpa's face.

"Today you got a special treat coming," he told us all. "Today I'm going to tell you the story of Santa and Pete."

"It's a Christmas Eve story," Maya said, understanding.

"I try to tell it every Christmas Eve."

"Well, how come I haven't heard it before?" I asked.

"Couldn't do it for a few years. Before that you were too young."

I sat there, ready for the story to begin. At the next stop, though, which was near Macy's, so many people got on—and not only people but also their packages and their groceries and their gifts—that I couldn't see my grandfather anymore, let alone hear any story he might tell.

"You would think that I loved waiting to the last minute to shop," a woman with pearl drop earrings and a hairy bear of a coat complained as she squeezed her way onto the bus. "It seems I'll never learn."

At every stop, more last-minute shoppers packed themselves in. One lady's humongous purse kept swinging and nicking my ear. Then when I moved my head, she took up that space, too.

My grandfather seemed to be batting a thousand, though. By now, two filled shopping bags rested beside his fare box. Talk about a basket catch! Except that a shadow had begun to move in over the bus as the sky turned a steely gray. Outside, a wintry fog pulsed from the noses of people walking down the street.

"Looks like the first snow of winter," someone said as the flakes began to fall. Not those little nothing flakes that hit the ground and die, but big fat flakes as large as silver dollars. So big, in fact, that I imagined that God held up a blanket in the sky until he'd gathered all the snow in heaven, and then yanked the blanket away. That's how quickly it all came down. Gobs and gobs of snow, gushing from the clouds. Perfect for a snowball fight had I been able to get to it. Instead, I pressed my face to the window, trying to see if God would answer my humble prayer—to make a blanket of snow on Earth that would last until I got home.

I thought all the regulars would be off the bus by the time we reached Battery Park, but they all stayed.

"I'm not going out in *that* weather," said Maya.

"Might as well head home," Mr. Levinson agreed.

So after what had seemed like an eternity of the bus inching downtown in the snarled holiday traffic, we finally turned around and headed back toward Harlem, which stretched roughly from 110th to 155th Street, and from river to river.

Suddenly the bus coughed, then it sneezed, and finally it stalled.

"Oh no," grumbled Professor DeFreese.

"I don't believe this," said Mrs. McCloud.

No one looked happy.

Grandpa tried everything that he could think of—inside the bus and out—to get it moving. Then I heard his sigh of defeat followed by a growling *"Dognabbit!"*

Frozen in
Our Tracks

ALL AROUND US, people abandoned their cars and trucks and taxis, turning the street into a parking lot. The blizzard had struck fast and furious, and now not a soul could see to drive, even if they could cut through the snow.

"No chains on the bus," Grandpa announced, sounding agitated, "so we won't be moving anywhere for a while."

A number of people asked to be let off. A second wave followed. Some said they wanted to try the subway, only a few blocks away, and soon only about fifteen people remained on the bus.

"Sorry, folks," my grandfather said again, rising from his seat. "I have to shut everything off. I'll run the heat for a few minutes here and there, but I don't want to poison you folks, and I don't want to burn out the engine."

When he turned off the lights, I grimaced. The charcoal-gray sky gripped the shoulders of the bus with the might of a giant. It was getting dark too fast. And now there were no lights outside. Both the street lamps and the store lights had abruptly gone out. Grandpa guessed that the storm had triggered a power outage.

I played tricks with my mind, trying to shake off my paralyzing fear of bats, vampires, and other creatures who come out to feed at night. I imagined peeking into the department store windows on Fifth Avenue: dazzling holiday displays with their streams of light, cheery Christmas carols, and animated puppets. I envisioned the brilliant bulbs spiraling up our Christmas tree back home, and the shine in my mother's eyes when my father played "My Funny Valentine" especially for her. Bright thoughts comforted me.

Outside, the city became hushed; people crept forward at a 45-degree angle through the bitter wind and blowing snow. I was glad not to be out there with them, even as several more passengers formed a third wave of people who decided to leave the bus and go it alone. Now only the regulars remained.

My grandfather went out to make SOS calls on one of the corner emergency transit telephones. Twenty minutes later, he returned, shivering and batting snow from himself, and then rubbing his gloved hands together, finally clapping them a couple of times to generate heat.

"Well," he said, pulling his hat off and snapping it against his thigh, "they know we're here." Steam escaped from the silver waves on his head. He stood there next to his fare box for a minute. Then he grabbed one of the gift-filled shopping bags and came over to sit beside me. With the bag near his right foot, he pulled out a tin.

"Might as well get to know one another a little better," he said. "Especially since I'm sharing my cookies with you."

A few of us chuckled as he passed the opened tin around. I'd never seen that kind of cookie before. They were rolled, with red jam in the folds.

"I made those," Rachel announced, taking two.

"What do you call them?" I asked.

"Rugelach," she said.

My grandfather took a bite of one and said, "Mmmmm. Thank you, Rachel."

Grandpa began the introductions.

"Some of you don't even know my first name," he said. "Funny

enough, it's Nicholas. Nicholas Mann. Next month it'll be twenty-five years I've been driving this bus. My wife always used to say that I talk better than I drive." He twisted his thick gold wedding band a half-turn on his finger. "You know the bit about me being a history buff, but I'm pretty decent at fixing up old houses too." Then Grandpa nudged me.

"I'm Terence," I told them, "and I like the Yankees, flying kites, and comic books about Martians—especially when the Martians win."

Aside from feeding birds Wonder bread, Maya Quick said that in her acting workshop, they always picked her to play the grand-mother, "even though I'm far too young for those parts."

Professor Anna DeFreese taught history at City College and often traveled to places that had mountains she could climb.

Albert Levinson, a tailor, smiled with pride as he said he could tell what size you wore "just by looking at you."

And his granddaughter Rachel Levinson collected angelfish and paper dolls.

Mrs. Alison Pearl McCloud talked a good while. She owned a hat shop, was a faithful member of the Abyssinian Baptist Church, and had been married to a wonderful man named William Acre McCloud, "until he passed—God rest his soul—two years ago."

As Mrs. McCloud finished up, I climbed into my grandfather's lap to stay warm.

"Need those antlers adjusted, do ya?" he asked. I leaned back against his chest as he rested his fists on my head, lightly twisting and turning them until he finally said, "There ya go, son."

"You didn't tell us about Santa and Pete yet," I complained, glad not to have all those people crowding the space between us.

"Santa and Pete," Grandpa said, his voice looming over us, as if he wanted people all the way in the next century to hear him. "Now, those two lived a long time ago, and in a way live still."

"Guess I might as well put this to good use," Professor DeFreese mumbled, pulling a red candlestick and a golden holder from her shopping bag and lighting the wick. She let drops of wax drip into the holder to form a seal between it and the candle.

I took a bite of cookie as Grandpa opened his thermos and poured a cup of coffee into the black cap. He offered some to everyone, but no one took him up on it except me. Unlike my parents, he let me have a big gulp, which went straight to my head and tap-danced on my brain.

"You want to hear about Santa and Pete, do ya?" His eyes scanned us all to see if anyone besides me and Rachel were truly interested.

"Looks like we got some time," said Maya.

"Maybe all night," agreed Mr. Levinson.

The soft beam from the flame gave all our faces a gentle glow. Now all eyes were on my grandfather, who had a little tickle in his throat. He seemed to feel every eye on him—the famous storyteller featured in the *Amsterdam News.* Then he was off, his words lifting us up and carrying us back to a time when Santa and Pete touched the world.

Santa and Pete

"TODAY EVERYBODY CALLS him Santa," Grandpa told us, beginning the tale. "But back then they called him St. Nick. And to look at him, you'd think that God was about to call him home. His face was ghostly pale. And though the thin white hair on his head no longer grew, his wild, fluffy beard seemed to stretch on forever. St. Nick didn't give much thought to his appearance—he'd wear anything as long as it fit, more or less. But he insisted on the softest shoes, made especially for him by a cobbler in Amsterdam. St. Nick had walked maybe a million miles and his feet hurt.

These days, people say you've lived a long life if you get to be eighty, ninety, a hundred years old, and St. Nick was more like ten times that old. But he got around. Had been almost anywhere in the world you could think of going, doing good deeds. Some people even said he performed miracles. If you looked him in the eye, though, you could see that he was tired.

Mostly, St. Nick was a gentle man, but he could be tough too. If a child misbehaved, he'd stuff a piece of coal in their stocking in a heartbeat. When it came to kids, the way he figured it, love and discipline went hand in hand.

You might think that children would be a little bit afraid of St. Nick, but that wasn't the case at all. They gathered around him, jostling one another to be the one to put their hand near his on his walking stick. Like I say, he looked old as dirt, but he had a deep-down bounty of goodness that people could sense. Kids especially.

Now Pete had a lot of mileage on him, too—although the years didn't tell on him the way they told on St. Nick. In fact, Pete was a handsome, young-looking guy with a dimple in his chin, or so I hear. And talk about shy! But when people looked into his soulful eyes, which were brown with flecks of gold, they trusted him right away. Life had taught Pete the healing power of compassion. He showed it in lots of little ways. Like at the prison in Seville—they only required him to whip up the same watered-down soup day after day, but when he had extra money he'd buy a hunk of meat or a chicken

to make the soup more hearty and flavorful. If he had a spare hour early in his workday, he'd bake up loaves of bread with fresh herbs and give each prisoner a healthy, buttered slice.

"Wait just one minute," Mrs. McCloud said. "Pete was in prison?"

"He worked there," Grandpa told her. "But St. Nick—he was actually behind bars."

"Well, that's no example to set for children," she said. "What was he in there for?"

"It was a case of right place, wrong time," Grandpa explained. "You see, he passed through Spain every year in late November. But this particular year, they said he was a spy and locked him up."

"Was he?" Mr. Levinson asked.

"Not in a million years," Grandpa replied. "By that time, St. Nick was so old he couldn't see straight, let alone spy on somebody."

"Well, that's different," said Mrs. McCloud, putting a pointer finger to her lips as if to say, Don't mind me—go on with the story. So Grandpa continued:

In the dark, in the cold, when all you've got to do is shove a bowl of soup under cell door after cell door, you probably wouldn't even notice the guy on the other side. But Pete noticed St. Nick. Gasped when he looked at him, in fact, because he saw stardust circling St.

Nick's face. The twinkle blinded Pete at first, like the flashbulb on a camera when you're not expecting it. Though he had intended to finish his rounds that evening, then take up his lute to practice, he found himself back at St. Nick's cell.

"What's a lute?" Rachel asked.

"That's like a lotta stolen money," I told her.

"No it isn't," Mr. Levinson said. "A lute is an instrument similar to a guitar."

"Now, Mr. Levinson." My grandfather caught his eye. "Gotta give my boy credit. There are at least two kinds: one makes music, the other makes friends."

The adults all laughed. When they finished, I laughed too, finally getting it. Grandpa hugged me and went on:

Then, without hearing him play a single note, St. Nick turned to Pete and told him, "Your music is a gift. It will bring joy to the world."

Pete's jaw dropped. He wondered how the old man knew about the instrument that the blind woman had given him. Maybe Pete *would* get good one day, but at that moment his playing sounded like two angry cats fighting over a single sardine. He had faith, though. And that was in his favor, because when it came to playing that lute, that's exactly what he needed.

"Where were you headed when the soldiers stopped you?" Pete asked St. Nick, gripping one of the iron bars of St. Nick's cell, feeling his fingers freeze and quickly letting go.

"Over to Holland," St. Nick replied. "I take my message there each year. They hold a big celebration, but I go to see the children."

"Sorry you have to miss them this year," Pete said.

"Not to worry," St. Nick assured him, "I'll be there." His prayers had begun to dissolve his fears.

Maybe it was the stardust, but Pete believed him. As they talked through the night, Pete admired St. Nick's towering spirit. And as Pete talked about navigating by the stars, and feeding three hundred people on a budget of spare change, St. Nick began to appreciate Pete's power to bring order to chaos.

So that's how St. Nick and Pete first became friends. To look at them talking that evening, you might have focused on their differences. One was black, the other white. One was a cook, the other a bishop, and so on down the line. But St. Nick thought it might be good to have a young, smart buddy along on his travels, especially now that his strength was waning. And Pete could see that St. Nick, known the world over for helping others, might be able to help Pete divine a greater purpose in life.

"How about some company on that journey, Nick?" Pete asked.

"I was thinking the same thing," St. Nick said.

"I tend to think that Santa and Pete were on a special mission," Grandpa told us. "That they were two of God's cherished angels. St. Nick, of course, being the veteran, and Pete just earning his wings. It was like God figured, Who better than those two to travel around teaching children how to get along so that they could grow up and straighten out this mixed-up world? But that is not to say that St. Nick and Pete always got along themselves. Not by a long shot.

Still, it worked out pretty well. Every year St. Nick and Pete visited Holland, coming to the aid of those in need along the way. While Pete would plan every single step, St. Nick might find himself a thousand miles from home without two nickels to rub together. At first they laughed about it, then it began to create problems.

Even with empty pockets, though, St. Nick never went hungry, and he always had a roof over his head. That's because people thought highly of him. But people feared St. Nick as well. They did their best to stay on his good side, and yet he wasn't fooled. He knew who was who. He had it all written down in his Book of Life, which he carried everywhere he went. It was five inches thick and filled with secrets about the past, the present, *and* the future.

Santa & Pete

Grandpa paused to take a sip of coffee, then went on.

As the patron saint of travelers, but especially sailors, brides, and of course children, St. Nick had a lot of people riding under his wing. Churches were named for him from Asia to Europe and also in what came to be known as the New World. But in Holland they clung to him most fiercely after 1492, when the Moor rulers were ousted from Spain. The Inquisition had started, and the new leaders were menacing Jews and Muslims. They even threatened to crush neighboring Holland because it practiced a different brand of Christianity. And eventually they did destroy a Dutch town named Haarlem. Throughout Holland, children went to bed each night fearful that they would not awaken the next day.

You should have seen Amsterdam when St. Nick and Pete arrived during those years. They could hardly step off the ship with all the children crowding the dock. The outpouring of love lifted them a foot off the ground. Then the children began to parade them around Amsterdam's canals, attracting more children. As the celebration passed by, people stopped conversations in midsentence to follow along. Shopkeepers left their shops. Farmers left their crops. The whole town came to a halt to join in.

Pete, who was normally bashful, felt surprisingly at ease in

Holland. He sensed the children's hunger for patience and encouragement. After the great feast, he would approach them one by one. Unlike Nick, he left the lumps of coal to the furnaces. He figured that every child had done at least one or two good things throughout the year, so he would ask each child to name a few for him. When they were done, he would say, "God is pleased," and then give them a book or a game wrapped with a ribbon. He told the children that he had high expectations for them all. Knowing how bad *he* was on the lute, he would give them credit for their potential rather than punishing them for their mistakes.

St. Nick was taken aback as he watched some of the most misbehaved children come around under the influence of Pete's praise. That's when St. Nick decided to leave the coal alone too and adopt Pete's way.

"People may think it's progress not to discipline their children," Mrs. McCloud said softly, "but I wouldn't call it that."

"There's a difference between discipline and crushing a child's spirit," Professor DeFreese countered from across the aisle.

"The wisdom is to know the difference," Mrs. McCloud answered back.

I thought everybody was going to get in on the debate. As a child,

I had a definite position on discipline—I thought it should be outlawed—and I would have been more than happy to share my opinion, but then the exchange between Mrs. McCloud and Professor DeFreese ended as quickly as it had begun, so Grandpa went on:

One year, when St. Nick and Pete went to Holland, they found a bunch of children missing, and the kids that were still there looked dispirited.

"They've gone to the New World, and they won't be coming back," said a little bitty girl.

As St. Nick and Pete looked into her sad, tearful eyes, it didn't take long for them to decide to set sail for the New World.

GRANDPA PAUSED, got up, turned the engine on, and flipped the heater switch, to let some warmth circulate throughout the bus. The lights blinked on for a few minutes too.

"When is this damn bus gonna move?" a sleepy voice creaked from somewhere in the back.

I jumped. Somebody screamed. We all held our breath and

looked behind us. Then I saw him: a little boy who appeared to be black like me, only he had a Spanish accent. My grandfather quickly scooted me over and rushed to where the child had popped up, about halfway back.

For a moment, Grandpa just stood in the aisle next to him, like he wasn't quite sure what to do.

"I've seen you in the train yard before," Grandpa said soothingly, as if the boy might be scared.

The boy said nothing.

"Shouldn't you be home?" Grandpa asked. "Won't somebody be worried about you?"

"I'm not going back," the boy finally responded, as he rubbed his eyes with his fists.

"Back where?"

"If I told you, you'd just try and make me go back. "

"I'm not making you go anywhere at the moment," Grandpa said. "I just want you to tell me your name."

"Raúl." The boy's voice sounded strained.

"Come join us, Raúl." The boy clasped my grandfather's hand tightly. When they got to the front, he appeared to be taller than me, maybe nine or ten years old, with matted, curly hair and brown-framed glasses that had broken and then been Scotch-taped back together in the middle. He wore a lot of clothes, but they stopped short of his bony brown wrists and ankles.

Grandpa sat him down on the same bench as me, but with a space between us. Then he put his blue bus driver coat over the boy's shoulders. I felt more anxious than ever. Once Raúl settled in, and let go of my grandfather's hand, I got up and let Grandpa sit in my seat so I could climb back into his lap.

When Grandpa offered the boy cookies, he munched down four of them in the time it would take the average person to eat one.

"Why don't you give him a few of your baseball cards to play with?" Grandpa said to me.

I searched through my deck twice and found three players that I could live without. I grudgingly handed them to the boy.

Everyone on the bus watched Raúl as he sat with his legs open, laying the cards down side by side, again and again, as if he could simply deal himself a new hand. He was quiet for a while, and then suddenly his eyes clouded up. He put his hands over his face.

"I want my mother," he said.

"Where is she?" Grandpa asked.

"In the graveyard."

"What about your father?"

"Locked up," he said through clenched teeth.

My grandfather rubbed his back.

Maya reached out her big hands and beckoned to him. "You can sit with me."

But Raúl pulled away and turned, pushing his face into the hard seat back as if no word or touch could ever reach the place within him that needed comforting. While the rest of us looked forward to being home, warm and dry, he seemed to hope that this moment on the bus might stretch on indefinitely.

Grandpa took his handkerchief from his back pocket and dabbed the boy's eyes.

"I ain't crying," he insisted, but he didn't push my grandfather's hand away.

"Yessiree, Santa and Pete," Grandpa said, as if he wanted to take the attention off of Raúl so the boy could collect himself.

$Ship$ of $Fools$

$\mathcal{B}$ACK IN St. Nick and Pete's time, you were limited to getting around by foot, horseback, or boat, Grandpa told us while folding his hanky and giving it to Raúl. Although St. Nick traveled all the time, Pete, except for those annual pilgrimages, stayed around Seville. Often, he thumbed through the journals of Christopher Columbus, which were stored in that city at the Archives of the Indies. The maps alone made Pete long to see more of the world.

Still, neither he nor St. Nick was eager to tackle the New World. It was so far away, and besides, people who had made the voyage said getting there was like being "hog-tied in a sack of misery." But St.

Nick and Pete had their minds made up to see the other children again. And besides, word had gotten back to them that trouble brewed in the New World. They thought together they might help.

Right away, Pete started to prepare for the trip. He gathered everything he thought he might need. He packed as many of his books as he could, plus his lute and a bunch of warm clothing. On the way to the dock, he shivered in the cold drizzle as he stopped to buy figs and oranges, dried meat, and crackers, which he pushed down into what little room was left in his three leather satchels.

At the last minute a fellow passenger came up to Pete, anxious to sell off his sheep so that he would have money for his trip. Pete figured the numbers in his head: With a dozen sheep, he and Nick would have all they needed for food and clothing, and even some to trade when money got sketchy. And he would be helping a fellow passenger to boot. Once the two men shook on it, Pete dug into one pocket after another, finally coming up with a combination of money, two rare books, and a thick, warm shirt to trade for the sheep.

As St. Nick and Pete approached the ship from the shore, the *Witte Haen* had the markings of a luxury liner. It sat high up on the North Sea, its smooth amber wood gleaming and curving around from bow to stern with Dutch orange, blue, and white flags flapping at both ends. Three rows of sails puffed in and out like Dizzy Gillespie's cheeks when he took a solo on his trumpet.

Icy black water lapped up the sides of the ship, not quite reaching the cast-iron side cannons, which were always at the ready in case of a showdown with another ship. Near the rear, the builder had painted on a mascot, a fat, white hen—which is how the ship got its name. That hen was so plump with pride that she looked like she had just laid the golden egg, or knew where to find it. That made sense, since her job was to go around the world, plucking golden eggs from the nests of other countries and bringing them home to the queen and to private investors.

Pete's baggage loaded him down as he made his way onto the ship, while St. Nick stepped lightly, boarding with the clothes on his back. The book of verse Pete had given him and a small box to protect his wooden teeth at night were tucked in his pockets. Under his right arm he carried the Book of Life, and in his left hand he held the reins to four white Arabian horses, which a Spaniard had insisted he take as payment for restoring peace in his troubled family. As everyone got on the boat, St. Nick stood there looking around as if he was confused. That's when a young stable boy came through and took both St. Nick's and Pete's animals for safekeeping, giving each man a wooden claim check with a number painted on it.

"Gentle," Pete said to the stable boy, who ignored him, using his whipping stick liberally as he walked the creatures down to the accommodations for four-footed guests.

Once everything and everyone was on board, St. Nick and Pete found themselves amid a tight clutch of motley passengers. They all kept their eyes glued to the shore, most of them wondering if they were making the worst mistake of their lives. Maybe they *could* earn lots of loot in the New World, but the Old World still looked pretty good from the deck of the *Witte Haen*. Besides, anything could happen in the three or four months it took to make a winter's passage. Storms and disease were common on the open sea, and surely at least one or two people wouldn't survive the trip.

"I have a bad feeling about this," Pete announced as he surveyed the ship, which proved to be as dirty on the inside as it was sparkling clean on the outside. They were leaving on December 7, and this in itself meant it was impossible to make it to New Amsterdam in time for Christmas, the next big holiday.

"Not to worry," St. Nick assured him, not noticing all the frayed nerves around him as passengers settled down, supplies were put away, and orders were shouted to get the boat moving. By the time the two men had collapsed in their little side-by-side cots, with barely enough room to stretch out, St. Nick could see things more clearly: The shipping companies made plenty of room for cargo and gunpowder. The officers lived well, too. But they squeezed the run-of-the-mill passengers into the leftover space, to take in a little money on the side.

Nobody bathed too regularly back then, and nobody hosed the animals down much either. Then there was the muck and the mess, the drowned rats, the old food, and the dank water that washed up in the part of the ship where they put stones for balance, so the vessel didn't tip over on them. But oh the odor! Those lucky souls who didn't become downright sick tried to keep their minds off the horrible conditions by playing board games or singing songs from home.

Now, as if all that weren't bad enough, the ship's cook, a thick man in dirty pants with a cherub's face, made matters worse. His job was to watch over the ship's food supply. The *Witte Haen* had only enough to take it the length of the trip, and maybe not even that far. The cook was supposed to keep the food from spoiling or getting eaten by rats. You'd think he'd pay close attention, but you'd be wrong. In fact, he could hardly pull his lips off a bottle to stir a pot.

The cook wasn't the only big drinker either. Pretty soon, he and the ship's navigator teamed up for swigs. They'd get together early in the day, toss back a few shots, and sneer at the suckers who'd spent their money to travel on the *Witte Haen*. Not long after, every meal started to arrive under thick, suspect sauces, and the boat started swimming in circles. Talk about sinking spirits. It makes sitting on this bus—even in the snow without much heat—seem a little brighter, doesn't it?

"The way you describe it, Mr. Mann, sounds like St. Nick wasn't, you know"—Maya looked at me, Rachel, and Raúl—"wasn't, you know, playing with a full deck."

Her comment reminded me that Raúl still had my baseball cards. I wanted to snatch them back, but I knew that would cause more trouble than it was worth.

By then the snow had covered the ground so thickly that you couldn't see where the sidewalk ended and the street began.

"I was wondering something similar, Mr. Mann," Mrs. McCloud said. "I mean if St. Nick was a saint and he had all those special powers, why would he let all those poor souls suffer?"

SOMETIMES THINGS GET worse before they get better, Grandpa told us, letting Mrs. McCloud's question hang in the air.

And the morning that St. Nick got called to pray over two young women's bodies, before the captain ordered them buried at sea, was the lowest of the low. The two women had come down with some kind of fever, and they went quickly.

Pete couldn't stand it another minute.

"The ship is not aligned with the stars," he said to St. Nick, almost shouting, as if he wondered whether the old man could still hear. "If we continue on this course, we won't make it to the New World at all. I'm going straight to the captain to offer myself as a navigator." And he did.

Meanwhile St. Nick prayed. Together they helped the *Witte Haen* surge ahead in the right direction.

Now, you might ask why they didn't do that *before* the two women died. But what you have to understand, Grandpa explained, is that they worked *with* God, not against Him, and when the Lord is ready for you, you've got to go. On the other hand, Grandpa added, you can't underestimate the spiritual power of the two men either.

The excited buzz spread. People started feeling hope. The food still arrived under those mysterious sauces, but at least the passengers felt they had a shot at getting where they were going.

"We seem to be moving very fast for winter," said Frieda DeWitt, a frail woman with a soiled bonnet. She had come to St. Nick two days before and asked him to perform the marriage ceremony for her and a man she had met on the ship. The man's wife had died and been buried at sea on the previous voyage, and now he had five kids to raise on his own. Frieda had been headed to New Amsterdam to live with her sister and brother-in-law but thought it might be even better to have her own husband to protect her in the New World.

"I'll need him," the woman told St. Nick, who knew differently. But again, he did not interfere with destiny.

"Godspeed," Pete said as he and St. Nick stood watching the thick pieces of ice break up and clear in the water just ahead of them.

St. Nick smiled, showing his awkward wooden teeth.

Pete smiled too.

Soon, birds started swirling overhead, and the passengers could see schools of fish darting around under the water. Then little bits of twigs and leaves started bobbing about the boat. It wasn't long before someone ran up and down the full length of ship shouting, "Land ho! Land ho!"

Of course that was old news to St. Nick and Pete. They stood near the gangplank, just waiting to get off that funky piece of ship.

GRANDPA PAUSED to take a few sips of creamy coffee. I watched the hypnotic cycle of the thermos cup coming to his lips and moving away.

"That woman on the ship was like my mother," Professor DeFreese said with a heavy sigh. "She married young, thinking things would be better for her that way." Professor DeFreese took off her glasses and dug around in her shoulder bag.

"Here you go, dear," Mrs. McCloud said, handing her a hand-kerchief from her own purse.

"Thank you," the professor said, wiping her nose with the hanky. "It's funny," she continued, "because my mother spent her whole life wiping *our* noses."

"Why is she crying?" I whispered into my grandfather's ear.

"The story made her a little sad," he explained, then he kissed the top of my head.

"She was tied down with seven children and a husband who could only get work maybe eight months a year," Professor DeFreese continued.

"What kind of work did he do?" Rachel asked.

"Construction. And they can't work when the weather is bad, so my father could be out of a job for months at a time. . . . Mother patched our clothes together so many times, everything we wore looked like a quilt." At that she laughed again. "And to this day, I can't be in the same room where beans are being served. By the time I was six, I'd eaten enough to last me a lifetime."

I stole another glance at Maya and saw her wipe her eyes too.

"I bet there were good times as well," Mr. Levinson said.

"There were!" Professor DeFreese smiled at him.

"Whenever anyone had a birthday—which was almost every month—Mother made the most delicious cakes with pudding in the middle.

"And Poppa took us fishing. We thought it was just for fun. We didn't know he did it for survival."

She took a deep breath and let it out slowly.

What Professor DeFreese said seemed to get everybody thinking about how they connected to the story, and every once in a while one of us would speak up and talk about a piece of the Santa and Pete tale that related to our own lives.

It seemed to me that to bring people together in this way, my grandfather had to be as special as St. Nick and Pete.

New Amsterdam Blues

PETE GAVE ST. NICK a hand as they stepped off the ship that morning. Though they couldn't see New Amsterdam's town crier, he stood at the top of a fort a short distance away, his piercing voice stopping the men in their tracks.

"It's nine o'clock and all is well!"

You couldn't tell it, though, by looking at Frieda DeWitt. She turned back and glanced at St. Nick and Pete one last time, offering a final wave of thanks. But her new husband paid her no attention and yanked her to hurry her up. They marched head first into the wind, right along the dock leading into town.

"If you're going to be my wife, you're going to have to move fast," he said. "I'm barely surviving as it is in this miserable colony. Time is money."

Most of the other passengers got off the ship, took a deep breath, and rushed into the fray. But for the longest time, St. Nick and Pete stood in the same spot on that dock, taking in the wooden and stone military fortress around the first settlement of homes, the people whizzing by like they might miss something, and a bunch of thrown-together little houses that made New Amsterdam look like a city without a plan.

Dutchmen in black hats and white collars and cuffs, women in black dresses with bleached or colored aprons, and thin bonnets over their hair passed by, but St. Nick and Pete also saw lots of other folks—Africans, Jews, French, Italians, and Asians. In this tiny town there was an array of different faces and cultures, and both St. Nick and Pete got to thinking, Maybe this really is some kind of new world.

St. Nick's eyes scanned the passengers as they began to blend into New Amsterdam. Finally, he caught sight of the newlyweds as the older groom tugged his young bride deeper into the crowd.

"At least she's warm," he said, catching the very last glimpse of Frieda DeWitt as she disappeared into the market wearing the buff-colored shearling coat he'd given to her as a wedding present.

"Only now it's you who's freezing, Nick," Pete said.

"I wanted to make the time she has left as comfortable as possible," St. Nick explained, shivering.

"The time she has left . . ." A whiff of the animals broke Pete's concentration as they came clopping up out of the hold of the ship, sluggish from the trip. He had prayed for the creatures every few hours. Suddenly, the man who had sold the sheep to Pete rushed up to him, before Pete could find out what St. Nick had meant.

"They survived remarkably well," the man commented. He had a jumpy left eye. "You were lucky we made the voyage so fast."

"No, *you* were lucky we made the voyage so fast," Pete told him.

"I don't know how you did it," the man said, counting the sheep twice to make sure they still added up to twelve. "I've *never* been so successful bringing sheep over."

Then Pete and the man watched as the dirty dozen bolted past them, running beyond the dock, onto the dusty Broad Way—the busy main road—and into the market, where soon they could hear people screaming. Every few seconds something crashed.

The sheep seller turned away from Pete with a smirk. Maybe this Moor had gotten the animals safely to the New World, but there was still a chance to steal a few back, he thought, if he hurried into the market before Pete got there.

"What possessed you to buy all those sheep?" St. Nick asked, finally walking forward with his mannerly horses.

"What *possessed* me? Try hunger, try cold. If it were up to you, we would have left Holland with no money, no animals, and no plan. I know God provides, Nick, but we're still on Earth."

With that, Pete handed his freezing friend a pair of pants and a shirt to add another layer to the ones he already wore. St. Nick fumbled as he slowly pulled on the extra woolens. Pete watched, shaking his head. "I'm always the one who has to figure everything out," he complained.

"Well, then, make sense of those sheep," St. Nick told him, "before they turn this town on its head."

"Watch this," Pete said, his mood lifting as he gave St. Nick a light punch on the arm. The old man stumbled for a moment, before Pete caught him and steadied him. Then Pete put two fingers to his mouth and blew. It seemed like there was nothing to hear, and yet everywhere those sheep had scattered—one of them eating into a bale of hay for sale, another one just now knocking over a vendor's table of pots and pans, a third one twisting itself up in the long skirts of a woman buying baby potatoes—every last one of those sheep stopped what it was doing, turned, and ran on back toward the dock. In three or four minutes, Pete had the whole lot rounded up.

"THAT WAS A NEAT TRICK with those sheep. But what I want to know is why'd St. Nick give up his coat, Grandpa? Especially if he knew she couldn't use it for long." It was cold on the bus, and I could only imagine how much colder it must have been in the New World.

"Well, son," Grandpa said, "sometimes it's the things we take for granted that bring happiness to others."

I looked over at the cards in Raúl's hand, and the handkerchief in Professor DeFreese's.

"It doesn't have to be big, just thoughtful," Grandpa said.

As he continued the story, I began to question more, like why had people really come to the New World? It sounded as though everyone was in such a rush putting up houses, getting settled, and trying to make money that they might not have even realized what they needed themselves. And what could St. Nick and Pete, who had their own problems, do for them?

Finally, St. Nick and Pete began to walk toward the fort, hoping to find a place big enough for them to sleep in and a place to house their animals for the night. The captain of the *Witte Haen* heard them discussing their dilemma while he checked off the crates of linens and crystal as the workers stacked them on the dock.

"I've got just the place for you," he told them over his shoulder.

"Tell us about it," Pete said.

"You go through town and into the woods, not far from the Hudson River. Nothing fancy, just a stone barn, but plenty big enough for each of you to stay out of the other's hair," he said, studying Pete's turban, "and of course to shelter your animals. Got a fresh couple of bales of hay in there too."

It sounded perfect, except for the price. Pete asked more questions about the place as he watched the dockworkers' long poles jab into the thick layer of ice that had just frozen around the *Witte Haen.* A second crew of workers prepared to roll barrels filled with beaver pelts onto the ship to take back to Holland, while a third wave of workers got ready to load lumber.

Pete turned back to the captain with what he thought was a more reasonable offer, but before he could get the number out, St. Nick said, "We'll take it."

Pete fumed. The man wanted nearly all the money they had on them. All Pete's money, really, since St. Nick always traveled so "light."

"One last thing," the captain shouted to them as they walked away. "Keep your wits about you. The soldiers and the Indians are on the brink of war."

"W H A T   W A R ? " Maya asked

"The war between the Indians and the Dutch," said Professor DeFreese, nodding.

"They went to war?" Mr. Levinson asked.

"And it all started over a peach," Grandpa explained. "But don't worry," he added, "I won't leave that part out."

The friendship between St. Nick and Pete took a downturn around that time too. Pete had had it up to here, Grandpa said with his hand indicating his neck.

"Maybe we should have given the captain the sheep too?" Pete snapped. "And maybe thrown in the horses, huh, Nick, since it's Christmas Eve?"

"We could go back and do that. It's not too late," St. Nick told him, continuing in the direction the captain had shown them. He knew the deal had angered Pete, but it wasn't that much money and anyway his feet hurt and he wasn't about to stand around arguing with the man. St. Nick would darn near give anything away—except for the Book of Life—knowing there was always plenty more.

They made quite a scene, that group, Pete and St. Nick fussing back and forth on the horses, with the rest of the animals running around them. As they moved toward the barn, they looked like a one-ring circus.

They began to cover some territory, though, moving beyond the bustling Broad Way, beyond the Wall, and finally, a short distance into the frontier, where trees suddenly shot up over their heads—some bare, some evergreen. The temperature dropped, but St. Nick warmed up a little.

After another half mile or so, they came upon the stone barn. Frozen, rotten apples littered the ground. A few hundred feet to the northwest, they saw the mighty river.

Pete silently whistled, and the animals flowed easily into the barn. He and St. Nick worked together to feed and water the creatures. It was fortunate that hay figured in the price, but the drafty, leaky barn still got Pete mad every time an icy drop of water fell on him or a frigid pocket of air blasted him. He jabbed wood into the stove, building a small fire.

St. Nick gently placed the Book of Life on the floor of the barn and slid down beside it, resting his aching back against a cold brick wall. He fell asleep instantly. He'd felt old for a long, long time. But now he began to feel ancient, as if every move he made was by God's will alone.

Pete looked at his friend, napping in the makeshift seat of straw. He pulled a blanket from one of his satchels and draped it over Nick. Then Pete took out a book of spiritual verse—like the one he'd given St. Nick. After reading awhile, he closed his book and got up. They had lots of work to do.

"So," Pete said loudly, trying to awaken St. Nick on the sly.

The old man opened his eyes and found himself nose to nose with a sheep. He nudged it away.

"We've got a lot to prepare for tonight," Pete said, banking the fire. "Shall we get moving?"

"Yes," said St. Nick, still bone-weary and scrambling to his tender feet, "let's."

"SOUNDS LIKE PETE was always frustrated with St. Nick," Maya observed.

"And often St. Nick was frustrated with Pete," Grandpa told her.

"It can be hard to travel with people," Mrs. McCloud said. "But then again it can be even harder to leave them behind." She fiddled with the clasp of her purse as she spoke. "My grandparents came to this country because there weren't enough jobs in Jamaica. And they had to leave my mother and her brother behind with relatives. It took a few years before they could save up enough to send for them."

Talk of children being sent for stirred Raúl. Perhaps he wondered if somebody in his real family might send for him. But after a minute or two, he just sat back and rested his head against the seat.

"My mother knew the sacrifice was for her, and a lot of good came out of it," Mrs. McCloud went on. "But she never got over her feelings of abandonment."

"I know how that is," Maya told Mrs. McCloud. "I was an orphan." She said it almost casually, as if it were simply a fact and not a painful truth. "I'd always imagined that my mother had left me on a church step with a tear-stained note saying how sad she was that she couldn't raise me. But if there ever was a note, then it must have blown away."

The candle flame steadied itself again, giving her face the warmth it might have had if we were sitting around a campfire, toasting marshmallows.

"I've chosen to forget a lot of my childhood memories, and yet there are some that I wish I had, like being held, or someone drawing a line above my head on the kitchen wall to see how tall I'd gotten since the year before. But I'm here," Maya said softly, as though she'd accepted the way things turned out.

"Why is life so hard sometimes?" I whispered into Grandpa's ear.

"Because it helps us appreciate when times are good," he whispered back.

I looked over at Maya, who had her eye on Raúl. But he didn't budge.

It Can't Be. . . .

*T*HE ROCKY VOYAGE had shaken the horses to their core, so Pete brushed their coats for a long time, trying to calm them. Then he hitched them to a sleigh he found just inside the barn. Finally, he and St. Nick climbed in and headed down to take a look at St. Nicholas Church. Pete wanted to see the house of worship named for his friend.

St. Nick, on the other hand, knew of hundreds of churches that had been named in his honor. As always, he felt humbled, but he preferred to stay in the barn to rest and pray, rather than taking the bumpy ride into town. On second thought, though, he didn't think the Book of Life was really safe in that leaky barn with all those animals around, so he figured he'd go along with Pete to find a place within the church to protect the book.

"What's so big about the book?" Rachel asked.

"Only God and St. Nick know for sure," Grandpa told her. "But sometimes a lucky person might get a peek at what was in it. Most times, though, they didn't even remember what they had seen."

"A mystery," Mr. Levinson said.

"Exactly," Grandpa responded.

So during their run back to town, the village, which had been so packed before, looked almost deserted. St. Nick didn't notice. He just sat back with his eyes closed and enjoyed the breeze through his fine hair.

The only people Pete saw along the way were a group of African men with massive arms in shirts drenched with sweat as they made planks of lumber from trees. A Dutch master ate a plain boiled potato as he supervised their work.

"It's twelve o'clock!" The town crier's voice gripped the island like a wrench tightening around a washer. But this time, he didn't say whether all was well, and his voice trembled.

St. Nick and Pete rode into the fort, completely unaware of the woman in a rainbow-colored shawl racing after them. She had just run down three flights of stairs, and out the door at the base of the

Great Windmill, which ground wheat for flour and hops for beer.

Four women—two slaves from Africa, and two indentured servants from Europe—paused briefly to look out the window and down at their by-now out-of-breath supervisor Maria.

"Sinterklaas and Piet!" the woman called after the two men, using their Dutch names, as she pushed open the gate and ran through the white picket fence that bordered the mill.

"Sinterklaas and Piet!" she called again. Still they didn't hear her. Out of breath now, she stopped, took in a gulp of air, and yelled, "Sinter and Piet!" That time they heard her.

Pete pulled the sleigh to a stop, shifted the reins, and turned to face her, slowly steering the horses around.

"I can't believe it's you," she said. "I worked for a Dutch family, when I was a slave girl, and that's all I hear: Sinter and Piet, Sinter and Piet. And here you are!" She gasped for air in her excitement. "Sinter and Piet."

That's when she saw the brown, leather-bound book sitting by St. Nick's side.

"Is that the Book of Life?" she asked, her eyes dancing between the old book and the ancient man like a hummingbird fluttering between buttercups.

"Some call it that," St. Nick said, resting his wrinkled hand on the volume. He knew that the book often made people afraid—especially the part about the future—and when they asked him about it, he tried to find a way to soothe them.

"Make good each day," he told Maria, "and the future rights itself."

"For true," she responded. "Then one day I will fly back to Africa just like a bird."

"Angola?" Pete asked, because her dark, diamond-shaped face reminded him of people he had met from that country.

"Maria D'Angola," she said, telling him the name she had been given. Lots of people from Angola had that same name. It meant Maria from Angola, and stood like a gravemarker over her lost African one. But Maria hadn't come to talk about that. She had approached them for a special reason, and then she needed to get back to work.

"Now, you will find that every Christmas Eve at my house is a very special supper. My family, we come together and tell the stories of how we were in Africa. Oh, please come this night!" She put her hands together as if in prayer.

St. Nick felt the pinch of time. It was a thoughtful invitation from a good woman, but they had so much to do before nightfall. He needed a few hours, at least, just to rest. He started to mumble

that they would try their very best to be there, when Pete said, "We'll come!"

This time it was St. Nick who got vexed. Here's the great planner Pete, he thought, acting as if the night would go on forever.

"Wonderful!" Maria exclaimed. "That does my heart glad." Then she began to give them directions to her house in the Greenwood.

"So when you arrive," she concluded, "just ask someone or look out for a house with barrels across the front. Even better, just follow the good smells. And be careful," she added. "It's gotten real bad between the Indians and the soldiers."

St. Nick knew what terrible things had happened, Pete had a feeling. Maria assumed they knew nothing and told them the whole story: an Indian woman passing through an orchard had picked a peach, but she hadn't lived to eat it. The Dutch farmer who had killed her had said that the Indians had eaten so many peaches that he didn't have much of a crop left, and the woman picking one more was the last straw. Now the Indians had retaliated, dragging more than a hundred Dutch men, women, and children from their homes. All were believed to be dead.

"Killed them all," Maria said. "It's the worst thing, so be very careful."

"A hundred people?" Mrs. McCloud exclaimed.

It Can't Be. . . .

"That poor woman," Rachel said. "For a little ol' peach."

"The colony was already poor and struggling," Grandpa told us. "But now people were at one another's throats. I won't leave that part out, either."

So the two men said their goodbyes to Maria, and then moved on toward the fort as a light snow began to fall. St. Nick took off the shirt Pete had lent him and put it over the book. The raw air snaked through the thinner shirt he wore underneath.

"Let's hurry to the church," he urged Pete, offering a silent prayer for New Amsterdam.

The horses pulled the sleigh into the fort, and both men were surprised to see not a single, solitary guard or soldier at the gate. They did see the governor's house to one side. A big place, but nothing spectacular. And while the barracks for the soldiers appeared to be on their last legs, the church rose up in all its glory. It was easily the most beautiful building on the island. St. Nick and Pete could see the steeple even from the barn they'd rented, but it was different to stand right next to it and witness for yourself how its blue slate roof reached so far up that its steeple appeared to puncture the passing clouds.

St. Nick and Pete tied their horses to a dark wood hitching post just outside the church and climbed out of the sleigh. Pete steadied

St. Nick, just as the doors opened and the Reverend Edward Bogart stepped out, buttoning his overcoat as though he were on his way somewhere. He stood tall with a wide face and puffs of brown hair over each of his ears but bald on top. As the doors closed, St. Nick got a glimpse of the interior: hand-carved oak pews, silver candelabra on either side of the altar, and walls the color of fine lace.

"Good day, visitors," the Reverend Bogart called.

Pete handed St. Nick the book, which he tucked under his arm.

"Good day, minister," St. Nick responded.

"I have just one question," the reverend piped up, with a bit of a chuckle in his voice. To him, they looked like the pair in the Dutch fairy tales. "Are you two here to play Sinter and Piet for the children?"

"We're not here to play anything," Pete told him.

"Good," the reverend said. "I'm sure you'll find that in this village, the children believe in no such pair."

"So you yourself don't believe in Sinter and Piet?" St. Nick asked.

"Once upon a time, when I was a boy," he said, "but when I became a man I put away childish things." Then he lowered his voice. "Though word is quickly spreading through town that you really are those two," he said, eyeing them.

"People say that," Pete replied.

"All the time," St. Nick added.

The reverend looked around the fort, wondering if the governor might be anywhere about—or anyone who might get the wrong impression. He cleared his throat, then spoke softly again: "If you *were* Sinter and Pete, you would be fourteen hundred years old, wouldn't you?"

"Possibly older," St. Nick said.

"Speak for yourself," Pete corrected him. "I would only be maybe half that age. Or younger, perhaps. But then, who's counting?"

The more he tried to pin them down, the more foolish the reverend felt. Yet he couldn't help himself.

"I," the reverend whispered, touching the tiny gold cross on his neck, "am a child of God who believes in miracles. And as such, I believe that God could make of you—or me—whoever would please Him. So it would only be a minor miracle for Him to make you Sinter and Piet."

"That is a relief," St. Nick said, "because we just might be who you say, after all. But on a more important note"—he changed the subject, wiping his damp head with a handkerchief—"I have a very special book that I need to be kept safe and dry, and I thought you might do that for me." He pulled the great volume from under the borrowed shirt.

The Reverend Bogart's eyes grew wide. He knew of the Book of Life. Had always longed to see it for himself. It couldn't be . . . and yet he couldn't take his eyes from it.

The snow fell even more heavily. St. Nick swept a few flakes off the book's brown leather binding.

"Reverend Bogart," he said, "would you look after this book?"

"How did you know my name?" the reverend inquired. "Although I suppose you could have asked anyone."

"What I'm *asking*," St. Nick said again, more forcefully this time, "is if you would look after the book until tomorrow."

"May I look *at* the book?"

"You may not," the old man said, growing more annoyed by the moment. "I'm simply asking you, as one man of God to another, if you will do me this kindness—and *that* is it." He placed the book in the minister's hands and began to untie the horses. "We plan to be back tomorrow around noon," St. Nick told him.

"But tomorrow is Christmas," the reverend protested.

"Ay, that it is," said Pete. And then the two men climbed back into the sleigh and took off.

"THE MINUTE they left, I would have had my nose all up in that book," I said.

"But St. Nick trusted the Reverend Bogart." Mrs. McCloud looked me in the eye.

"Yeah, but he didn't stick around to *make sure* he didn't look, so to me that would be St. Nick's problem."

"Not really," Maya said. "If you tell somebody a lie, who's done wrong, you or the person you told it to?"

"I bet a lot of people would *say* they wouldn't look. . . ." I gave up, realizing that adults always felt they had to say the right thing, whether they did it or not.

"Speaking of lies," Mr. Levinson said, a fire smoldering in his voice, "how many lies have been told in the name of Christianity?"

"Lord, have mercy!" Mrs. McCloud exclaimed. "Well, I don't believe this."

Nobody did. The bus got real quiet. It was the kind of quiet where nobody knows what to say, and everybody's afraid of what's going to happen next.

"I mean, this is quite an engaging story, Mr. Mann, and I'm sure it's quite popular. Just to listen to it, I'd have to say I like it. But as a Jewish man, I must also say that something's missing."

What could be missing? I wondered.

"One of my ancestors wrote an early account of New Amsterdam," Mr. Levinson told us. "In it he talked about how the Jews had been forced out of Brazil, and arrived in New Amsterdam with only the clothes on their back—only to find more trouble. One evening, in fact, as my ancestor brought home a menorah to his family, a couple of the town's so-called upstanding citizens attacked him. One snatched the sacred candle holder from his hands, while the other one beat him, stole his money, and ridiculed his faith."

Mr. Levinson gripped both his cane and his granddaughter's hand tightly, yet he never raised his voice.

"So, Mr. Mann, we mustn't pretend that a nice Christian story suits everyone. It seems to suggest that there's only one way to worship."

Rachel shifted in her seat as though she couldn't have been more uncomfortable. I think I knew how she felt—maybe she wished her grandfather could be a little less Jewish for a moment. There were plenty of times when I wished my parents wouldn't make such a big deal about being black. But they insisted it was an important part of who I am.

I thought Mr. Levinson had finished, but then I saw him tap his cane.

"It's even harder as we try to raise our children." He looked around at each one of us. "We want them to know that it's okay to believe what we believe. That it's okay if they don't embrace Santa Claus. And not only okay, but that is their right under God to worship according to their own beliefs."

Maya's shell-bead bracelet rattled a bit as she ate a cookie that she'd held in her hand awhile.

"I heartily agree," Grandpa said. "All faiths and all people should be able to reach up to God in their unique way. Certainly there were people in the colony who would have tried to run you out, and that's partly why I tell this story. They failed to bridge the gaps between all different peoples, but we still have a chance."

"What is faith, Grandpa?" I whispered in his ear.

"It's the thing inside that helps you hold on till help arrives," he whispered back.

A Reindeer for
Your Horses

REVEREND BOGART WOULD have in-
tervened if he had seen anyone being attacked in New Amsterdam,
my grandfather told Mr. Levinson. But a man does not a whole town
make, and one of the most unsavory characters had the most power.

We'll get to that, Grandpa assured us. We don't want to lose track
of St. Nick and Pete, though. After meeting Reverend Bogart, the
two set their sights on finding something to eat before going back
to the barn.

Every few blocks a tavern appeared, but oddly enough for a
Saturday afternoon, most were closed. St. Nick and Pete were discussing why that might be, right about the time they came upon two

boys fighting in the middle of the Broad Way. The children looked to be about eight and ten years old.

"Everywhere I go, *you* go. Quit following me," the taller, heavier boy shouted. Then he stuck a leg out and tripped the smaller child.

"Nobody's following you, fat face," the younger boy yelled, whipping around and throwing himself at the other child's legs. Then they were both on the ground, rolling in the new snow, making mud and throwing punches.

"Halt," Governor Stuyvesant ordered them as his official carriage made the turn from Stone Street onto the Broad Way. Carefully, he stepped from the shiny black coach, pulled by two dull-gray horses. One of the governor's officers scrambled out of the carriage to take his place beside his boss.

For the moment, though, the governor fussed like a harried father trying to get his children to mind him. One of his feet was a wooden peg, so he steered clear of the squabbling.

"I said stop it! What if those savages were to come out right now? You boys'd be so busy squabbling, you wouldn't even notice. I've ordered everybody in the colony to stay indoors. Now I come out and see my own children defying me."

St. Nick and Pete's sleigh drew closer to the scene.

"Governor Stuyvesant has his hands full with New Amsterdam and little Cain and Abel there," said St. Nick, chuckling. "All year long, one punches the other, then the other punches him back."

"Wait till they see us," Pete said.

Finally, St. Nick and Pete slowed to a stop and asked the governor if they might help. Pete thought he might be able to defuse "the bomb." But when the children saw St. Nick and Pete, they hopped to their feet as though nothing had ever happened. One licked his finger and smoothed a lock of hair behind his ear, while the other tried to untangle his clothing. Still, they couldn't cover the fact that they were filthy from head to toe. The younger child even had a bloodied nose.

"Let me help you up, dear brother," the older boy said.

"Oh, yes, thank you, brother of mine," the younger responded.

Then they turned, exactly at the same moment, and said, "Oh, it's Sinter and Piet. Well, hello, Sinter and Piet."

But St. Nick and Pete kept their eyes on the governor, who snorted and snarled and appeared angrier than ever.

"There is no Sinter and Piet!" he yelled. "All day long, I'm having to clamp down on heresy. Those Quakers shaking like the devil's own; those Jews with their oily Hanukkah; and those Muslims following that snaky writing in the Koran. Now my own children are making gods of fairy tale characters."

Stuyvesant grabbed his boys by one ear each.

"Well, let me tell you"—he forced his words through his teeth— "this colony is on the verge of collapse. We have no time for fun and games. Now, run along and get the sheriff." Then he shoved them forward, which made them howl as they flew halfway down the hill toward the town's only open tavern.

"Can't rely on the imagination of children to run a town, now, can I?" Stuyvesant tipped his wide-brimmed hat so that he could size up the two visitors.

"So I'll ask you two," Stuyvesant said, "who are you and what is your business here?"

"My name is Nicholas and this is my friend Pete. We're here by the will of God."

The governor winced at St. Nick's words. He couldn't stand there on that leg of his much longer, so he had to make a decision. There was nothing illegal if these two men wanted to play Sinter and Piet, but he could slow down their progress.

"Now, about these horses," Stuyvesant said, admiring the shiny coats of the stallions. "Where did you get them?" He closed his eyes for a moment and bit his lip. Then he rubbed his thigh above the wood.

"I must ask you to step out of your sleigh," the governor said.

Now that he had a moment to look the animals over, he saw how exceptional they were and he wanted them for his army. His supplies were running low, and earlier in the day an order of gunpowder had arrived from Holland soaking wet.

"Do you have weapons?" the governor asked.

"None except our bare hands," Pete said.

"You're no match for the savages on this island, I'll tell you that. They just killed a hundred of our people. Now, let's just say you were to happen upon one of those savages this afternoon. How would you two defend yourselves?"

"We have no quarrel with the native peoples," said Pete. He stepped out of the sleigh, followed by St. Nick. "We're not expecting any trouble from anyone."

"Failure to anticipate is the undoing of many a dead citizen." The governor shifted all his weight onto his good leg. Then he closed his eyes again and gritted his teeth. "I'm going to have to hold those horses for now. We'll supply you with a suitable pack animal until it's time for you to leave."

A Reindeer for Your Horses

"You can't take our horses," Pete protested.

"Executive orders," Stuyvesant said. "Trust me, it's for your own protection."

They didn't trust him one bit, but it seemed futile to fight.

Down the hill, the boys, still cupping their ears, huffed back toward their father. They ran a few steps ahead of the sheriff, who dragged a small, loaded-down reindeer. When the boys again reached their father, he put a hand on each of their backs and gave them a shove.

"Now, get on home," he said, "and quit your bickering."

"You heard what he said," the bigger boy shouted directly into his brother's ear.

"Ow!" the smaller boy cried out. Then he turned around and yelled back, "Don't you tell me!" And they argued and punched each other all the way down the road until they turned a corner, out of sight.

"You needed me, sir?" the sheriff asked, dragging his reindeer. The man blinked a lot, his gray eyes shifting from person to person.

"*They'll* be needing your little friend, there," the governor informed him.

"Sir?" the sheriff asked, not understanding.

"I haven't got all day," the governor exploded. "Unpack the animal and give it to 'em."

The sheriff lifted the side packs, which were joined in the middle by a wide piece of leather.

"Reindeer's named Rudi," he said, reluctantly handing over the rope that led to the animal's neck.

"But it's a female," said Pete.

"What's so wrong with the name Rudi?" The sheriff looked from St. Nick to Pete to St. Nick again.

"So," Stuyvesant said, staring at Pete with a harsh glare, "when are you gentlemen leaving New Amsterdam?"

"Tomorrow, around the noon hour," St. Nick told him.

The governor pulled out a tiny scrap of paper, wrote "I.O.U. four Arabian horses" on it, then signed the debt with an unreadable scrawl.

"Here," he said, "you can claim these horses at the governor's mansion tomorrow."

Then he turned to the sheriff and said in a voice he thought St. Nick and Pete couldn't hear. "Get four more soldiers armed and on these horses. Tell 'em to get on up to the Haarlem barracks."

St. Nick missed it, but Pete heard it word for word. With that, the officer and the sheriff galloped off.

T H E   T O W N   C R I E R sounded as if he'd swallowed a gallon of dust. "It's two o'clock"—his voice forced out the words—"and the governor has ordered all to finish their business, take to their houses, and bolt the doors."

"The horses are in danger," Pete said.

"They'll be all right," St. Nick assured him.

They dragged their sleigh halfway down the hill and tied the poor reindeer to the hitching post in front of the tavern that the sheriff had come from. Before the two men wandered into Wolf's Place, a roadside eatery, Pete reached into his pocket and gave Rudi a handful of hay, which she lapped up.

The sawdust that was spread over the dirt floor gave the air in Wolf's a fresh, sweet boost, though it was no match for the musty scent of the men dressed in heavy, dingy clothes and drinking tall steins of beer. St. Nick and Pete sat at one of the wobbly wooden tables and ordered hot apple cider and bowls of beef-bone soup. It was all they could afford.

"Looks like tonight's the night," a man with a nasty cut over his eye told another fellow, who looked almost too young to be in a tavern. To Pete, the young man's cowlick appeared to have a bit of stardust sprinkled in it.

"For every one of us they killed, we oughta get a hundred of them. They need to learn their lesson once and for all. That's the only solution." Then he held up a stein, and the younger man matched him. But they were both afraid as well as tipsy, and some of their beer splashed out of their glasses.

"Better drink it slow, Wendt," the cut man said. "We've still got to make it up to Haarlem tonight."

"Why does Stuyvesant have to plan an attack for Christmas Eve of all nights?"

"It's not about Christmas Eve, it's the last night of the Indian powwow—or whatever they call it. If we don't get 'em now, they'll be off the island by morning."

"My wife's in a delicate condition," Wendt said, sounding reluctant.

"We've all got our troubles," the cut one replied. "Just make sure you get yourself up to Haarlem tonight with the rest of us."

St. Nick and Pete stayed only long enough to finish their food and drink, then they were on their way to prepare for the night's special deliveries.

"Well, well, well," said Pete as they stepped out into the twilight.

"The more the merrier," said St. Nick.

In just a few minutes' time, seven male reindeer had gathered around Rudi, each turning his head this way and that, trying to attract her attention.

"The Lord toils in mysterious ways, His wonders to behold," Pete said, smiling as he silently commanded the animals, hitching them to the sleigh. The two men climbed in and pointed the eight sets of antlers toward the barn. The ride couldn't compare to being pulled through town by a fleet of fine horses, but the contraption turned out to be not bad in a pinch.

The candle flame blew sideways as if a gust of wind had hit it.

"So *that's* how they got the reindeer," Rachel said, hopping out of her seat and doing the twist almost as well as Chubby Checker. "Wait a minute." She stopped twisting. "Girl reindeers have antlers?"

"That's right," Grandpa said.

"Rudi was a girl! Rudi was a girl!" Rachel taunted me.

That revelation really tore me up. In those days, to me any victory for a girl was surely a loss for boys.

"May I have a cookie, Mr. Mann?" Rachel asked.

"Only if it's no trouble," Mr. Levinson told my grandfather.

"None at all." Grandpa sent me over with another box of cookies, which had been wrapped as one might present the gift of a shirt. I stuck my tongue out at Rachel.

"That's not nice," Maya said.

"What happened?" Grandpa asked.

"Terence stuck his tongue out at Rachel."

"Say you're sorry, son." Grandpa's voice rose to full strength. It gave me goosebumps.

"Sorry," I told her, even though I didn't mean it. Then I took the cookies and offered them around.

"Would you like one, Raúl?" I said it politely, as if my mother might be listening in.

He grabbed a handful of cookies and dropped his head against the seat back again as he snapped off a piece of one of them.

Maya's eyes rarely left him. Though she rested her hands in her lap, I knew that, in a way, they still reached out to him.

The Magic Woman

"**W**HAT I CAN'T figure out is why St. Nick and Pete didn't just stop somewhere and buy St. Nick a coat," Maya said. "It was the dead of winter, wasn't it?"

They did try to buy St. Nick a coat, Grandpa told her. In fact, they took a few of their sheep to market that afternoon. The animals, which had been out of control getting off the boat, now fell right in line when they heard Pete's silent whistle.

But as he and St. Nick and the sheep entered the market, they saw that it was a skeleton of what it had been that same morning, with almost everyone packing up to go home for fear of attack. There were a few people still haggling, and a butcher sawing through thin meat and thick bone.

The Magic Woman

When a big foul gust belched through the market from the tannery, St. Nick pulled a handkerchief from his shirt pocket, covered his nose, and started to amble out. Pete continued to walk around, but he didn't see any coats. After he'd wandered a good while, he and the sheep went outside to where St. Nick sat in the sleigh. Then Pete climbed in too and the pair started to make their way up toward the barn again.

Now, don't kid yourself. It was cold out there. But when Pete tried to turn off the road toward the barn, where they could make a fire in the woodstove and get warm, the reindeer ran on.

"Did you see that?" Pete asked.

"Looks like an Indian woman, and she's trying to hide," St. Nick replied.

"I wonder if it's some kind of trick," Pete said. He tried to slow the animals down again and turn them around. But they kept going at full speed. Several hundred yards down the way, they came to a sudden halt, right where the woman had been.

"Where did she go?" Pete asked.

"What does it matter?" St. Nick responded, "Let's get ourselves back to the barn. I can barely keep my eyes open and I've caught a chill."

Pete gave a whistle, but the animals wouldn't budge. Then the snow stopped, and sunlight filled the sky. That's when they heard a slight rustle to their right.

A female form with a reddish-brown, moon-shaped face peeked from behind a tree.

"You're back," she said to St. Nick.

"Mmmmm," he responded. He didn't have the foggiest idea of what she was talking about.

"We've been expecting you," she said, startled that this might be the fulfillment of a two-thousand-year-old prophecy.

Usually, St. Nick got a reading on people the moment he looked at them, but when he saw her, there was nothing, not a clue. It was as if her edges were blurred. Would he and Pete be taken hostage? he wondered.

"The white man with the large mouth from the sky. Yes indeed, we've been expecting you."

"She says you have a big mouth, Nick," Pete teased. He sensed the woman meant them no harm.

"Why are you hiding behind the tree?" St. Nick asked. Now when he looked at her, he knew instantly that she was connected to the young woman killed for picking the peach.

"We're not supposed to be here," the woman said, as if there were

others behind her. "We are up the trail here in a secret place. I came to get you."

"Why?" St. Nick asked.

"For our celebration of Grandmother Sun. If we thank her properly, she will return with her warmth and her crops."

Pete looked at St. Nick. Beyond the road in either direction, thick, untamed forest sprouted up, mixing the sunlight with shadows of leaves and branches. Behind the blurry woman, a little reindeer wandered out of the woods and over to the pack, striking up an immediate friendship. The animal carried tobacco leaves in deep pockets that joined in the center and lay on either side of its narrow flanks.

"I'm Ramapo," the woman said. She tickled the animal on his head, right between the antlers.

"Perhaps we can ride together up to Haarlem for the celebration. My people have been waiting for you."

Pete and St. Nick looked at each other again. Still, neither said a word, yet each could tell the other thought it would be okay. Pete wondered how close the Haarlem barracks and the Grandmother Sun festivities were to each other.

"It's four o'clock"—the faint voice of the town crier came

through the trees—"and the governor orders *everyone* to return home and bolt your doors at once."

"Let's go," Pete said.

The reindeer ran north briskly with the sheep clopping alongside. Soon they polished off that forest in no time flat. Then they rode by the stretch of barns and farms just beyond the Haarlem sign, until they came to the end of the St. Nicholas trail. Finally, at a rocky cliff that stood high over a small river, they found a clan of the Lenape tribe. But once they stepped from the sleigh and turned back to the woman, she had disappeared.

On the rock, a girl stood watching them. She might have been all of ten, and the boy with her maybe eight. Both burned cones of sage, as well as tobacco leaves, waving their arms through the air and letting the smoke drift to the sky.

"You're Him," the girl said.

"Who would that be?" St. Nick asked.

"Him!" she said, as if the one word should explain it all.

She and her brother wore brown beaver coats. She had a round, cinnamon-colored face with high cheekbones and a thick braid. Smooth purple shells had been woven into it. The boy looked just like her. And both of them shone from the heavy layer of bear fat rubbed onto their faces to keep them warm. The girl stared at St. Nick and Pete as though she could hardly believe they were there.

"Please come," she said, running down the hill. There was something in her pockets that made a clicking sound.

Her words mingled with the wind as she ran while telling them of the legend.

"A man with your beard and your mouth came to us once and we all danced. He flew into the sky, but he said he was coming back one day."

"Where's Ramapo?" St. Nick asked.

"Who?" she said.

"The woman who brought us here."

"I didn't see any woman with them, did you?" the girl asked her brother as they rounded the rock at its highest point.

"No."

Pete turned back briefly, craned his neck, and counted the reindeer twice. Eight. The ninth reindeer had disappeared as well.

"Coming?" the girl asked again.

She ran to the edge of the cliff rock and then disappeared, as if she had jumped.

For a moment, St. Nick and Pete stood stock-still. A rosy gold sunset fanned over the river to the west. The children's free spirits and the beauty all around them made them breathe easier, although they didn't completely relax.

"There's your church." Pete pointed toward the steeple some ten miles down the way. In fact, they could see the whole island from up there, how vast the forest was, the huge boulders, the rushing waterfalls.

The girl ran back to them, laughing and inviting them to follow along. She took them through a passageway that wound them under a big rock overhang, where a ledge appeared. Pete held St. Nick's arm as they slowly snaked down into a clearing below. Inside a long tent with an arc ceiling, about thirty people sat in a circle—men on one side, women on the other, each wearing a coat of animal fur. Their song sounded as if it sprang up from the core of the Earth. One drummer played a heartbeat rhythm, while a little girl jumped up and danced, sprinkling music with the bells jingling from the laces of her baby moccasins.

Finally, an older woman with a puffy face and a wooden pipe wedged into the side of her teeth came outside the tent and stood before St. Nick and Pete. She looked questioningly at them.

"I'm Nick and this is Pete," St. Nick told her.

"I'm Shawnee," she said. And what is the name of the person who brought you here?"

"Ramapo," Pete told her.

"So the spirit moved you," she said with a half smile.

The girl who had first greeted them now stood behind the woman, whose thick salt-and-pepper hair fell loosely around her shoulders. Her long brown dress, taut at the hips, was adorned with purple porcupine quills at the neck. Because the girl stood directly behind the woman, she seemed to disappear again.

"We children have seen these two in our dreams," the girl said, her voice rising over the woman's shoulders.

"I thought you only saw *him*," Pete said. "The big-mouthed one." He laughed.

"You *and* him," the girl said to Pete.

"So you saw the penny-pincher too?" St. Nick asked, teasing Pete back.

Then the woman reached back, resting her hands gently on the girl's head. That's when the woman turned and whispered something to the girl, who ran off, grabbing the arm of the boy. When they returned minutes later, they held gifts in their arms.

"We made this one for you," she said, helping St. Nick to slip on a coat that glowed red in the setting sun. It was made of the finest, softest fur he had ever felt, and it fit him perfectly.

"And this is for you," said her brother, presenting Pete with a suede tunic similar to one Pete's father had worn. The children helped him slip it over his head, and then Pete stood there, slowly running his fingers over the intricate beadwork that ran in two parallel columns down the front of the garment.

Then the two men sat down to listen to stories, including the one about how life started for the Lenape people—on the back of a giant turtle, which stretched itself out to form the land. There was a lot that the two men didn't understand, and yet a good deal that needed no translation at all. The children were burning sage, tobacco, and sweetgrass, and the whole clan serenaded the sun, charming her to come back and bring spring with her.

When it was time to leave, St. Nick and Pete offered the Lenape woman the sheep as a gift. Though he knew it might make her angry, Pete decided to ask her something he'd been thinking about all afternoon. He knew the missing people weren't dead—at least not yet.

"The Dutch people you have, what do you plan to do with them?"

"We don't know," she said, glaring at him. "They're safe for now. But they've killed so many thousands of our people already, what's a hundred of theirs?"

"More pain," Pete said. Then he let it be for the moment, helped St. Nick into the sleigh, and climbed in after him. The men waved to the Lenape as the reindeer dashed away.

"All over one little peach," Mrs. McCloud said. "What a shame."

"And once something like that gets started," Mr. Levinson added, "nobody wants to be the first to say, 'Okay, enough already.'"

"That's true," Professor DeFreese said, looking at Maya.

"Very true," Maya added.

Grandpa's voice began to sound hoarse and tired, as though maybe *he* wanted to say, "Okay, enough already." He looked outside. Every now and again, we would hear a car shush by, its headlights buried by the snow blowing over them. Some drivers managed to avoid all the haphazardly parked cars, but more than once we heard the muffled crash of metal slamming against metal.

"I don't see a soul out," said Mrs. McCloud, cupping her hand in an upside-down U to peek out the window. "What if we're here all night?" she asked.

"Now, don't you worry," my grandfather reassured her. "They know we're here. They're coming for us."

I suspected as the captain of this ship, though, he worried more than anybody.

"You all might want to get up and stretch your legs," he suggested, maybe not sure whether anyone was still listening to his story. He had been talking a long time. Only a third of the candle remained. And the appeal of sitting around it on a bus, eating cookies and pushing the world away, had started to wear thin.

Everybody but Raúl got up. The adults kicked out their legs and complained about how much they had to do before Christmas Day. I challenged Rachel to a race to the back of the bus, which Grandpa vetoed. As we moved about, everything outside appeared still, and from the comfort of our living rooms it might have looked like a winter wonderland.

After all the stretching and chatting and gazing out, we all went back to our same old seats. Grandpa started talking again, but not about St. Nick and Pete. I thought he might single out one of his ancestors as some of the others had. But instead of the past, he talked about the future.

"I was just thinking about the whole notion of family," he said, resting his chin on my shoulder. "That if we can let go of what we think it should be, then maybe we can be happier about what we have.

"Friends," he said finally, "sometimes make very good family."

Pete's Gift

$\mathcal{I}$T TOOK THEM a few hundred years to jell as friends, but during that first trip to New Amsterdam, Pete and St. Nick started to appreciate each other. As he had when they'd first met in Spain, Pete reflected on how faith had freed St. Nick from worry and fear. And St. Nick was reminded of how much safer he felt with Pete sorting out all the details.

You might think they would get right to work when they returned to the barn that evening, but St. Nick needed a good long nap first. Violet light slanted in through the barn's high windows as he lit a lantern and held it before his sleepy eyes. There was a pallet near the far window that he had found earlier, so he kicked away some loose sprigs of hay to set the lantern down. Then he laid himself down on the makeshift bed. For a while, he tossed and turned until he found just the right spot. Then he slipped into a sleep so deep and sound that it seemed he might never wake again.

Pete read for a while, then tuned the strings of his lute and played for a bit, groping at chords. When a sheep wandered over and nipped at the strings, he put the lute aside, got up, and fed and watered all the animals. Outside, he made a fire and boiled water, which he used to wash up. Stepping out again, he put a wool blanket in the sleigh, took the few books he had brought with him for the children, and tucked them within.

When he reentered the barn, Pete heard St. Nick stirring. The air was filled with the most delicious aroma. Pete followed his nose beyond the dozing sheep and napping reindeer to the back of the barn.

"Is that chocolate I smell?" Pete asked.

"It's here to be smelled," said St. Nick.

Pete noticed a stack of tiny folded papers on the edge of the table, along with hunks of chocolate in the shape of alphabet letters.

"Ready?" St. Nick asked.

"As ready as I'll be," said Pete.

Between the two of them, they had only enough treats for ten or twelve children at the most. They carried modest gifts for Maria and her family as well, loading the sleigh and hitching the reindeer to it. Pete used his sextant and the stars to navigate the path northeast to Maria D'Angola's home in the Greenwood, a marshy area with massive pine trees. He looked to the sky, and felt a fresh rush of inspiration.

As they entered the small village, they discovered a scene straight out of sub-Saharan Africa, with its grass roofs, chubby Guinean sheep, and lean Angolan goats grazing along the way. Then Pete saw the barrels across a porch that Maria had mentioned, and the aroma of a home-cooked feast wasn't far behind. Before they could get out of the sleigh, Maria had thrown open the door and raced out.

"It's Sinter and Piet, everyone!" she screamed breathlessly over her shoulder to those in the house. Then she called to St. Nick and Pete, "I'm so glad that you have come. The whole family is here to welcome you."

Three small faces crowded the door, and behind the children stood their father, a big, strapping man whose large hands rested on their shoulders.

"These are our children: Little Manuel, Jacob, and Julia. And of course, this is my husband, Big Manuel."

The girl hid behind her father's legs.

Pete's Gift

"Come on out here and say hello," he told her, scooping her up into his arms.

"Go 'head, boys, say hello," he instructed them.

"Don't mind these kids," said Big Man. "Just you give them a few minutes and they'll be all over you."

"Come on in some more," Maria invited them, walking St. Nick and Pete into the two-room house, the biggest room being the kitchen, which spilled out into a dining area.

"This is my friend Janet Roosevelt and her husband Claus," Maria said. "And this is my little sister Christina, and her husband Wendt."

St. Nick and Pete caught each other's eye. They recognized the young man from the tavern. He seemed sober now, but antsy. He put a finger to his lips, as if he'd prefer that St. Nick and Pete not mention anything about what was said in the bar.

"Keep sipping from that cup, little sister," Maria told Christina, "then time'll fly and that baby'll be here before you know it." She turned to St. Nick and Pete. "The baby's already three weeks late. I'd be surprised if it doesn't arrive here walking and talking."

Christina, very pregnant and looking fragile, lifted the sweet, strong concoction to her lips and took a long sip. Wendt patted her back. St. Nick knew that she had lost two children already, and that this one might be in danger.

Christina's mother had died when she was born, and she feared that the same would happen to her. As they shook hands, St. Nick held on to to hers. Then he pulled from his pocket the chocolate initials NPD.

"Nathaniel Paul DeWendt," Christina whispered, suddenly ashen. It was the name she and Wendt had chosen for a boy. Then she looked up at St. Nick with a mixture of wonder and fear.

"He's going to have a sweet tooth. You'll have to watch that or he'll end up with a wooden smile like mine," St. Nick said, flashing his beige teeth.

He handed out gifts of chocolate and riddles to the delighted children. St. Nick wrote each message especially for the child who received it, sometimes helping them to be reunited with a favorite toy that had been missing, always suggesting that God knew the child and that the child might grow from knowing God.

The riddle for Maria and Big Man's littlest one read:

> Julia,
> To some they are rags,
> To you a doll.

Pete's Gift

If you miss Lizzie,

Look behind the mill wall.

Walk in faith.

St. Nick gave a scarf of rainbows to Maria to go with her colorful wool coat, and a whittling knife to Big Man. Big Man was surprised and pleased by his gift, since he had thought about taking up whittling just two days before.

To Janet, Claus, Christina, and Wendt, St. Nick gave chocolate initials.

Pete gave books to the children, and he tried to find the confidence in his heart to give the thing that he really wanted to share with everyone that night.

"Making ready for the big night must make you two hungry," said Maria, basting a large roast in a Dutch oven over an open hearth.

"Starved," said Pete.

"I've been nibbling on my own initials," said St. Nick, "and yet I'll be happy to eat."

"I haven't seen chocolate that fine since Holland," Maria remarked as she scooped rice into a bowl. "Where did you buy that?"

"Special order," said St. Nick, pulling her initials from his pocket and placing them in her hand as soon as she set the big bowl of rice on the table. There were more bowls, pots, and platters all around the kitchen. She started to put the food on the table. There was a big salad, kale and collard greens, a pot roast, a turkey, a ham, candied yams, green beans, and a gravy boat. Then she pulled a dish towel off an enormous cast-iron frying pan and cut the cornbread inside into wedges.

"Got a groundnut stew I made from a recipe back home in Africa too, if anybody wants to taste."

"I'll have some over my rice," Pete said.

After they'd eaten and the children had climbed all over St. Nick and Pete, just as Big Man had predicted, the group began to talk about the threat of the English taking over. Rumor had it that back in Britain they were so certain of victory that they had already started to call New Amsterdam New York. The family talked about the fighting between the Indians and the soldiers and wondered if it would ever end. They feared the worst was yet to come.

"Now I've got nothing against the Indian people," Wendt announced, resting his pale hand on his wife's deep brown one. "But this time they've gone too far."

"This is a party. Can we please speak of something else?" Maria said, lifting the basket of cornbread, which went all around the table but ended up in the same spot, untouched. People had helped themselves to plates of food, but no one had touched them.

"Eat up," she said. "I guarantee you, all the problems of the world will not be solved tonight."

Still, nobody budged from the topic.

After a while, Pete stood up and said he was going to get his lute.

Once outside, he looked the two horses over. The white one with black spots he recognized from the tavern. He untied it from the hitching post, silently instructed it to run, and watched it bolt. Then he grabbed his lute from a satchel inside the sleigh and headed back in. Though he had never played in front of anyone, he decided that he wanted to share the gift of song.

As he took his seat again, he placed the instrument on his thighs and held its neck with his left hand. Then he cleared his throat as quietly as he called to the sheep, and the heated conversation came to a halt.

At first the music sounded stiff, but everybody seemed so happy to hear it—particularly Maria, as she pulled Big Man close and then swung him out and they began to dance—that Pete felt encouraged to put his all into it. The chords wove together seamlessly. As new ideas popped into his head and emotions welled in his heart, his fingers translated. Soon the children, St. Nick, Janet and Claus, and even Christina (very carefully) and Wendt were up and dancing to Pete's spicy flamenco. He got so bold that he launched into songs that he'd never played before. He thought he didn't know them, but found out otherwise. A full hour later, when the final strum rippled through the air, the house crackled as if on fire. They all clapped and laughed and bubbled about how good they felt.

"If I knew how to make music like that," St. Nick said, giving Pete a pat on the back, "I wouldn't bother to make chocolate."

As he put his lute away, Pete felt the spirit of the blind woman still reverberating through the instrument. His heart filled with joy and gratitude in a way it never had before.

The excited chatter and laughter bounced off the stone walls even as a knock came at the door. But before Maria could walk the few steps to answer it, the door swung open and Jonas Zwick, the man with the jagged cut over his eye, stuck his face into the house. He was out of breath, as if he'd been running instead of riding a horse.

"Wendt, you in here?" He looked around the table at the black faces mixed with white faces, and then his eyes settled on Wendt's white hand resting atop Christina's brown one.

"Right here," Wendt announced, lifting the hand and wiggling his fingers.

"That's the problem," Zwick spat. "Governor wants us making tracks to Haarlem. I had a feeling you would be one of the stragglers. Come on, let's go."

"Go ahead. I'll catch up to you."

"We're shorthanded as it is," Zwick said, needling him.

"He says he's coming *soon*," Maria's voice sliced into their conversation. Then she rose and headed for the door, pulling it toward her. Zwick let go. "Get you something to drink before you're on your way, sir?" she asked.

He refused to answer, turning his back abruptly to her and leaving. They heard him gallop off, cursing into the wind.

"I guess I should go too," Wendt said.

Everyone turned to look at him and Christina. He faced her now, his blond cowlick fringy in the lamp light. Her thin black eyebrows crowded together over her full nose, and her round belly shifted slightly as the baby inside her moved.

Again, Pete saw stardust twinkling in the fringe of Wendt's hair.

"It's the Indians." Christina searched his eyes. "You're going up there for revenge."

Pete's Gift

"They committed a crime, Chrissy," he said softly. "I know what you're thinking. I don't like it either, but it's my duty."

He held her by her shoulders, pulled her to him, and then rocked her in his arms.

"Will our baby know its father?" she asked him. "Will he grow up to fight this same battle?"

"I'll be back" was all Wendt could think to say.

"Be safe." She wiped a tear from her eye before it could fall.

"Always," he assured her.

"We have to be going too," Pete announced, standing. He, St. Nick, and Wendt all made their way toward the door at the same time.

"Before you go," Maria insisted, "you have to try my doughnuts." She brought out a large tray of warm, sweet, puffy circles, and everyone dove in.

"People tell me I should sell them," she said, "to make extra money. Big Man and I are saving up to buy our children's freedom."

"I have no doubt you'll do quite well," Pete said between bites, savoring the memory of the day he had purchased his own freedom.

"I almost forgot," Maria said, and then she disappeared into the kitchen. "Let me give those poor little reindeer something to eat."

She put out a few pans of greens and rice. When they were done with that, she wanted to give them some nice fresh rainwater to drink. She had gathered it in one of the many pots lining the kitchen counter, but a few of those pots looked alike. In one she had brewed a clear but potent concoction. She kept its ingredients and powers a secret, using it only under very special circumstances. As she placed the bowls down before the animals, she had a strange inkling that in her hurry she'd quenched their thirst from the wrong pot, but she quickly dismissed the thought.

"Where's my horse?" Wendt shouted, as he stepped out on the porch.

"Maybe Uncle Claus's horse ate him," one of the children speculated about the brown stallion, which was licking his lips and straining against the hitching post.

"Hush up," Big Man told the child.

Wendt looked as if he might have a fit.

"Perhaps we could take you where you want to go," Pete offered.

"All the way to Haarlem with *that* sleigh and *those* reindeer?"

"You'd be surprised," St. Nick told him.

Wendt hesitated a moment, but with no other choice, he climbed into the sleigh.

Pete's Gift

"Same time next year?" asked Big Man, as the group stood around outside.

"If God wills it," said St. Nick, climbing in after Wendt as Pete steadied the old man's arm.

"Don't forget the music," said Julia, this time putting an arm around Pete's knee. Pete lifted the little girl and gave her nose a tiny tweak.

"Wait a minute," Maria yelled as she ran back into the house. She filled a pot with assorted meats, rice, yams, and greens and brought it out. "This is an old pot anyway," she said, tucking it into a burlap sack and setting it on the floor of the sleigh between Pete's and St. Nick's feet.

"Good luck, Sinter and Piet," Maria said, as the adults waved from the porch.

"Bye, Santa and Pete," the children sang—and that was the first time anybody called St. Nick Santa and Piet Pete.

"Say goodbye to Uncle Wendt too," she told the children. "Bye, Uncle Wendt," the kids said.

"Bye," he said, waving back.

And then they were off.

Santa & Pete

"WHAT DOES UNCLE WENDT have to do with Christmas?" Maya asked.

"When do they go to the North Pole?" Rachel wanted to know.

"And when do the kids take their picture with Santa and Pete?" I questioned my grandfather.

Raúl looked at Rachel and me as if he wanted to add something. I wondered if he would have any kind of Christmas at all.

"Uncle Wendt was on a mission too," Grandpa explained. "You'll see. The North Pole and all the picture-taking stuff came much later."

"Santa seems a little shaky to be doing all that running around," Rachel suggested. "That old man was falling apart."

"Rachel!" Her grandfather reined her in with the tone of his voice. "Show some respect."

"And what kind of gift is a song, anyway?" I asked. "That seems pretty lame."

"You give what you have," Maya said. "And to the right person, it might be just what they need."

Ready for Takeoff

"WE NEED OUR HORSES," Pete said as the sleigh ran north through the woods.

"Somebody stole your horses too?" Wendt asked.

"You might say that," St. Nick replied. He gripped the sides of the sleigh and the reindeer picked up speed. One minute they pulled this way, the next they switched up and yanked the other way. Finally, Pete decided that the animals should be placed in a line, with Rudi in front. Rudi's nose glowed as she blushed. All her life, she'd been underfed and overworked. Now she was being treated as though she was special. That made her run faster and faster, and the others ran just as fast to be near her. No doubt about it, Rudi had charisma.

"You're a brave man, Wendt," St. Nick told him, as the reindeer pulled the sleigh into swaths of the forest that had been cleared. It was 'round midnight, with darkness to match.

"I'm not feeling so brave," Wendt admitted, settling in between the two men. He worried about Christina. Maybe the braver choice, he thought, would have been to stay with his wife.

St. Nick was quiet. He just smiled, figuring the young man couldn't have been more than nineteen or twenty. Still, he could see that Wendt was earnest.

"What do you think, Pete?" Wendt asked. He was glad he didn't have to make the trek alone.

"You seem courageous to me," Pete agreed, steering northeast by the stars and his sextant. He marveled at the reindeer, which continued to run fast and nimble, even as he loosened the reins.

Wendt considered it. Maybe they had a point. Maybe not.

"Look at Stuyvesant," Wendt offered. "Now that's bravery—having his leg blown off in battle. He faced that. I could never . . ."

"That's something different from what is needed tonight," Pete told him.

Wendt became frustrated. He didn't know what St. Nick and Pete were trying to tell him, and he was anxious enough about what he might have to do. "Look," Wendt said finally, "I'm following orders here. I don't have to be a hero; I just want to make it back to my wife in one piece."

"What if I told you that the people you think are dead are not?" St. Nick asked.

"Then I'd say . . ."

"What if I told you *you* are the solution to this crisis?" Pete talked over him.

"What proof do you have that the people are alive?" Wendt asked.

"All the proof we need," Pete said. "And while you can assume that we are wrong, consider that we might be right."

"What if I don't choose to stick my neck out?"

"Then the day will decide itself," St. Nick said.

Wendt stewed as they leaped through the last bit of forest before the farms of Haarlem began to appear. Now he wished he'd borrowed Claus's horse and traveled alone.

"Do you know the way?" Wendt asked as they neared the barracks.

"Of course," Pete said.

But when the sleigh shot past the barracks, Wendt began to worry again.

"You said you knew the way and yet we just passed the barracks. I'm already late." Wendt looked over his shoulder, as if fixing his eyes on the two torches that marked the gates of the barracks could make the sleigh stop and turn back.

"Forgive me," Pete told him. "I should have told you that we have one stop to make first."

Even with a swell of moonlight, it was hard to see the great black rock. But it was as if Ramapo led them again, the reindeer stopping on cue.

"What's this?" Wendt asked as Pete and St. Nick began climbing out of the sleigh. The reindeer fidgeted in place, ready to dash.

"Shhhhh," Pete said to calm them down.

"It's the place where the Indians have their ceremonies. We were here earlier," St. Nick said.

"Are you crazy? We could get killed," Wendt whispered.

"They probably have more reason to fear us," St. Nick said.

Finally, Wendt climbed out of the sleigh. He was not eager to join Pete, who helped St. Nick ascend the rock, and yet he feared being left behind.

"Where does this lead?" Wendt asked, placing a boot on the base of the vast boulder.

"To the place where peace begins," Pete said, luring him on.

But when they got to the top of the rock, rounded the ledge, and began to inch their way down, Shawnee, the woman with the purple quill necklace, threw open a flap of the longhouse. Moonlight filled the circle before the house.

"Come no closer!" she said from the darkness inside. "There are people here and beyond who are prepared to fire."

"It's Nick and Pete," St. Nick told her. "We've brought our friend Wendt. He's a good man."

Shawnee bit her pipe and looked him over as though she wasn't sure.

That's when the girl and the boy who'd given them the coats ran out, and then more children followed. St. Nick and Pete pulled chocolates and fruits and books from their pockets and passed them out to the children.

The cries of a newborn rent the air.

"A new baby?" Wendt said.

"Three days old. She's my granddaughter."

Her words were drowned out by the voices of the soldiers spilling over the rock and cutting through the forest on either side of the longhouse.

"This is the moment," Pete said.

Wendt swallowed. He had never been so afraid in all his life.

"I have a baby on the way," he sputtered. "And your new one is only three days old. What can we do . . . now . . . together, to solve this?" Wendt asked Shawnee.

But she bit the pipe even harder now, not offering a clue. She thought of all the lives and the land that had been lost. The young woman killed for the peach had been her niece, Whispering Leaves. What about all of that?

"Before the others come, let's agree," he said.

"What do we get out of it?" the woman asked, pulling her pipe from her lips for a moment.

"We get to see our children run and laugh and live," Wendt said. "We get a chance at peace."

He could hear the heavy edge of Stuyvesant's voice, and the clops of horses' hooves closing in.

"I have it under control, Governor," Wendt shouted out of desperation.

"I'm here, sir," he yelled again, feeling a trickle of faith flow through his veins. "This is DeWendt, sir, and war has been averted. Our people are alive! Soldiers, hold your fire," he said, planting his feet firmly on the earth.

He looked into the woman's eyes not sure that this was true, but knowing that he had shown all the bravery he could muster.

"For the children," Wendt pleaded.

Ready for Takeoff

"Yes, for them," Shawnee finally agreed.

As the soldiers and the Lenape warriors crowded in, Wendt and Shawnee were in the middle of it all. Though *they* had agreed, with so much anger and firepower around them, anything could happen. But St. Nick and Pete had done all they could, so they stepped back and retraced their steps to the sleigh.

Pete signaled Rudi and the sleigh took off. More than running, it felt as if the animals were leaping. Big leaps, long leaps, and covering as much ground as the horses, maybe even more.

"What did Maria give those reindeer?" Santa asked.

"I was just wondering the same thing," Pete replied.

Santa and Pete raced through the night, zigging and zagging as they needed to reach each house. And at each home, they discovered that word of their visit had spread, since all the children had left hay and carrots in their boots for the reindeer. In one night, the animals ate enough for a week, but it didn't slow them down.

As they traveled from house to house, Santa's supply of chocolate, riddles, toys, and tangerines never ran out. And when Pete reached down for what he thought was the very last book, he found two dozen more.

"When you give freely," Santa said as they flew over the wall, "you enjoy abundance."

As they approached the Stuyvesant home, Pete wondered if Santa would make an exception and rain down a few lumps of coal through the chimney. Instead he gave the children their initials, wooden cars *and* riddles on folded paper.

The note to the older boy read,

> Nicholas.
> When you don't fight,
> You have already won.
> Open your fists,
> Life can be fun.
> You're special in God's eyes.

He got a special kick out of writing the poem to the younger boy:

> Bart,
> It's hard to be little,
> When the world seems so big.
> Find a way to be strong,
> Without being a pig.
> Love is the answer.

He dropped Nicholas's and Bart's gifts down the chimney, where they landed in the boys' stockings, which had been hung with care.

Even as they finished the last house, the reindeer showed no signs of fatigue or even of slowing down. The animals' leaps just grew longer and higher and higher and longer until they seemed to be . . . In fact they were! Well . . . I guess you would just have to say . . . Flying. They were flllllyyyying!

As they rose over the the village wall, Santa thought about the magic woman who had told them of the man with white hair and a large mouth in the sky. He remembered Maria and her desire to wing her way back to Africa. And he thought of how he had begun to love the wind in his hair.

"Oh, what a joy," he said, feeling free and light.

"What about the horses and the sheep?" Pete asked.

"I slipped the IOU and the key to the barn to Maria; she can share them with the rest."

"And what about the book?" Pete asked.

"We'll have it sent to us." And at that, Santa reached down and wiggled his fingers. In St. Nicholas Church, the Reverend Bogart stood poised to close the chapel doors and head for home. Suddenly, he witnessed the pages of the great book, which rested on the altar, riffling in a sudden wind from nowhere. He ran to the book and saw the massive volume pop open to the page where his mother's and his father's names were written, and below theirs his own, and his children's names and the names of . . . As he reached out to hold it down, it flew up as if being sucked through the roof. But the moment the book shut, the pastor couldn't remember what he'd seen.

Santa reached his hand down and scooped up the book, placing it by his side.

As they rounded the southern tip of the island, Pete put his hand out of the sleigh and pointed to the gathering of colonists and Indians. "I wish I could give them lasting peace, but that is something they will have to give to themselves."

"Shall we head for home?" Santa asked.

"Yes," said Pete, "let's."

And they did. In the first of many, many voyages around the world, they spread love, respect, joy, and the best chocolate you ever tasted.

"NOW, ON CHRISTMAS DAY," Grandpa said, "Santa and Pete weren't seen in town, but that morning, Reverend

Bogart looked north toward the rock, and saw a trail of at least a hundred men, women, and children walking down the St. Nicholas trail together."

Shortly afterward, Christina's baby was born safe and sound, and Wendt was there with her. And you might be interested to know that they named the boy Nicholas Peter DeWendt for the special visitors. All in all, it was the best Christmas ever in New Amsterdam.

Grandpa took a deep breath as if he had been talking forever. He didn't even bother to pour the last of his coffee into the cup, drinking it directly from the thermos instead.

"Can you tell the story again, Mr. Mann, pulleeeeeze?" Rachel asked. "I love it soooo much."

"Tell it again right *now?*" he said, as if he couldn't believe she was serious.

"Yes, now."

"I won't be telling that story again until next year," Grandpa said. "But feel free to tell it yourself."

"I think I will," Rachel said, jumping up for a quick reprise of the twist.

Raúl stirred. I suppose he anticipated the night drawing to a close.

Ready for Takeoff

"You might not believe me," he said to no one in particular, "but I'm not going back home."

"What's wrong with your home?" Maya asked.

"They don't want me. I'm just a check to them." He looked over at her.

"I know how it is to not feel wanted," she said.

We all watched, quietly, waiting to see what might happen.

He looked at her through his taped-together glasses as though he wasn't sure whether he should trust her, but it was getting late, and he didn't have many options.

"Can I come and sit with you?" she asked. "Like the way Mr. Mann is sitting with his grandson?"

Raúl looked over at me and my grandfather, and then back at her. He nodded.

Maya walked over and the boy got up, climbed into her lap, and settled in.

"Your butt must be as tired as mine," she said. "And my butt is really, really, really, really, really tired."

Raúl giggled. Maya provided lots of cushion.

Antlers on a Nightstand

$\mathcal{F}$IRST WE SAW the light. Then we heard a dull knock on the bus door.

"We've been rescued," Mrs. McCloud said, as if it was the saddest thing that had happened to her in a long, long time.

"Dang," I protested. As I hopped up, I took a bite of cookie and crumbs flew from my lips.

Grandpa climbed into his seat so that he could open the door.

"You all right, Big Mann?" A heavy voice burrowed into our spell.

"Just a little car trouble," my grandfather replied.

"Well, they sent me to get y'all."

"So you're Big Mann," Professor DeFreese said, winking. She held the candle for a while longer, even though Grandpa had turned on the lights. We all gathered our things and wished one another happy holidays. We hugged and laughed and promised to stay in touch and to repeat the ride the following year.

My grandfather waited until everyone was off, and then he slung his small duffel bag over his shoulder and took the two still quite full shopping bags up in his two hands.

"Ready, son?" he asked me.

Then we joined the others on the bus behind us, which took everyone as close to their home as possible, considering the roads were as bad as they were.

Before Maya got off the bus, my grandfather had a word with her.

"By rights I should call Social Services," he told her in a hushed tone, but he saw Raúl clinging tightly to Maya's hand.

"You have to promise me you'll call his guardian," he said. "I could get in a lot of trouble for this. But since it's Christmas Eve and he's so clear about not going back there, I'm going to trust you on this one."

"You have my word, Mr. Mann. I'll find out his guardian's name and I'll call." Then she and Raúl stepped off the bus.

"Wait," I said, running down the steps with a thick, soft scarf that I'd found in one of my grandfather's shopping bags.

They turned back toward me.

"Here." I wrapped the scarf around Raúl's neck.

"Thank you," he said.

"Come fly a kite with me and Basil sometime," I said. Now that he was leaving, I hated to see him go.

Professor DeFreese got off. Then Mrs. McCloud, who invited my grandfather to Christmas dinner if he didn't already have plans.

"He's coming to *our* house," I said, cutting her off, and feeling regret the second the words left my mouth.

"Well, I can understand that," she said, with a brave smile. But I could see that I'd stung her.

"I'm sorry," I told her. I even said it loud enough that she could actually hear me.

Finally, we dropped off Mr. Levinson and Rachel.

At the depot, I followed my grandfather through rows and rows of buses and into a little office, where he spent a half hour or so filling out a report on the incident.

Then we walked to his shark-finned black Cadillac a couple of blocks down the street.

"Help me pass out some of this stuff," he said, swinging the shopping bags out ahead of us.

We gave away more cakes and cookies to the people we saw on

the street than we had eaten that day. The only thing I remember Grandpa keeping was the bright red silk tie Mrs. McCloud had given him.

When we got down to our last cake, I said, "We should keep this one for ourselves."

Then he whispered, "What would Santa and Pete do?" So we gave it away as well.

During the drive up St. Nicholas Avenue, we enjoyed the cotton-soft quiet that only snow can bring. Colorful bouquets of Christmas lights strung overhead led us home. When I climbed the steps of our house and rang the bell, my parents threw open the door as if they'd been watching for us from the window for years. The living room blinked green, pink, and orange in the glow from the Christmas lights. The aroma of buttery sweets from the kitchen made me feel better about our having given all the treats away.

Grandpa explained the mishap to my parents, and I told them about Santa and Pete, the regulars on the bus, the good cookies, and the candle that had lit our faces. They smiled and nodded their heads as if my news was no news to them. I tried to tell them about the magic, but who could explain it?

We had a midnight snack of hot chocolate and peanut butter crackers, and then it was time for bed.

"I want Grandpa to tuck me in," I insisted when I heard him reach in his coat pocket and fish out his keys.

"And away you go," my father said, picking me up, kissing me, and then swooping me down and up in our game of airplane. Then he sent me for another dive, and pulled me up again so I could kiss my mother's cheek, and finally he landed me in my grandfather's arms.

Upstairs, Grandpa helped me into my pajamas. As I climbed into bed, I looked to the window to make sure no one was flying by.

"You're not going to sleep with those antlers on, now are you, son?" he said, sitting in the chair on one side of my bed.

"Can you help me take them off, Grandpa?"

"Now let me see here," he said, feeling around his pant loops. "I don't have my tool belt on me, but I'll see what I can do."

Then Grandpa twisted and turned his fists on my head until he said, "There!" Then he got up and walked around the foot of my bed.

"Let me set them on the nightstand for you, son," he offered.

I got down on my knees and said my prayers, including Maya, Mr. Levinson and Rachel, Mrs. McCloud, and Professor DeFreese

on the long list of people I needed for God to bless. Then I put in a special request that Raúl have a good Christmas.

Finally, I climbed into bed.

As Grandpa pulled the covers up under my chin, he put a finger to his lips and whispered, "Shhhhhhhhhh. I think I hear Santa and Pete."

All, Us, We

$\mathcal{M}$Y GRANDFATHER retired a few years after that Christmas Eve bus ride. But when I got to be a teenager, we got on the road again as he taught me how to drive. A great insurance policy for him, it turned out, since as I got older he often called on me on Saturday mornings to help him run errands. Eventually, I bought a convertible just because he got such a kick out of driving through Central Park with the top down.

We'd make a day of it, going to get his prescriptions and his peanuts from a man who sold them over on Lenox Avenue. We'd drop by to see his buddies, get some lunch, and argue about everything from politics to race matters to how to be a man and what to look for in a woman. On that last point, I listened closely, since

Grandpa had proved a winner in love twice in a lifetime. First there was my grandmother, of course. Then there was Mrs. McCloud, who ultimately won his heart.

We stayed in touch with Maya, who stayed in touch with Raúl. And to this day, he and Rachel remain among my best friends.

Over the years, Grandpa continued to tell me the story of our family, making sure that I had the complete picture. Then one day, he shared with me his belief that there is one person in every generation who is the keeper of the family history.

"That person has the responsibility and the honor to pass it on," he said.

"Do you think that might be me?" I asked him.

"Possibly," he said. "You will know when it's for sure."

One chilly day in early December, Grandpa died. He left me, among many other treasures, his basement museum. He had Indian corn, arrowheads, and wampum, the shell beads once used for money. There were also a lute and some carvings and masks from Africa. And from the Dutch, the wooden Haarlem sign he'd told me about when I was a child, as well as one baby clog.

One day, I went to the Schomburg Center for Research in Black Culture here in Harlem to gather information for my first book. I had been up nearly forty-eight hours straight, but I stayed until the library closed. The lights were being turned off as I put my reference books back on the shelf. That's when I stumbled across an unusual volume. It was so thick and old, I wondered what it could be. Then I noticed the brown leather binding and the brown string that tied it shut. I carefully rested it on an open space on a nearby shelf. It seemed ancient in the dim library light.

Inside, it was full of names, tens of thousands of them. Who could make sense of it all? Finally, I flipped to the middle and started surveying the names there. That's when I came upon the name of the Reverend Edward Bogart. I read backward from his name, finding all the people who came before him. Then I read forward to all those who came after him. Could it be that this book contained the names of the unborn?

Flipping forward through the book, I scanned names quickly. Then I saw it. My own name. Above it were my parents' names, and so on and so on—all the people in our family my grandfather had told me about. I turned back several pages, following the trail, and there I discovered something Grandpa had never told me: Pete's name appeared at the beginning of our family line. Suddenly I felt lightheaded, like someone or something had sucked all the oxygen from inside me.

I put the book back and sat down at one of the research tables just to catch my breath. When I went back to the shelf where I'd found the book, it was gone. I called the librarian over, and she said she'd never seen such a volume.

I searched every shelf near where I'd first discovered the ancient text. How had it arrived there? Where had it gone? Why had *I* found it? And were my children's names and their children's names there? I had a million questions, and yet I had to be content that not one would be answered—at least not in the way that I'd hoped. The words of my grandfather grazed my ears, "There is one person in every generation . . ."

So these days, I often scoop up Maria and Manuel and put them in the car for a Saturday-morning ride. Whenever I do, they know there's a story coming their way. The years go by so quickly, and sometimes I feel that they'd rather play with their friends or their computer games. Or maybe it's plain old lack of interest. After all, I was the same way at their age. But when they do tune in, I secretly study their eyes. Maria's only nine, and Manuel's only seven. Still, I can't help but look to them to see who will be next to carry on our family legacy.

One of the last things I remember my grandfather telling me is about an African belief that as long as someone is alive to call your name, you never die. So we continue to speak the names of our an-

cestors and to remember what they shared with us. In that way, they will live forever.

We count Santa and Pete among our people. To this day, when I think of one, I naturally think of the other. I learned a lot from them. About friendship, teamwork, doing for others, and having the faith to push past the differences that can divide us, even when it makes us uncomfortable. At Christmastime, we put Santa and Pete side by side under the star at the top of our family tree. The kids will tell you in a heartbeat that they belong together. And, I have to believe, so do we all.